THE MUKESH AMBANI WAY

Biography & Success Secrets

A.K. GANDHI
SUJATA SINGH

PRABHAT PRAKASHAN

Published by
PRABHAT PRAKASHAN PVT. LTD.
4/19 Asaf Ali Road,
New Delhi-110002 (INDIA)
e-mail: prabhatbooks@gmail.com

ISBN 978-93-5562-681-3

THE MUKESH AMBANI WAY: BIOGRAPHY & SUCCESS SECRETS
by A.K. Gandhi *&* Sujata Singh

Edition
2025

Price
₹ 400 (Rupees Four Hundred Only)

Printed at
SS Japan Art, Delhi

Author's Note

India is a land of promises, and there is no dearth of opportunities for a person who has talent, takes risk and likes to plan things well. This is the reason that we can see a number of people excelling in different domains of life: sports, science, technology, business, spirituality, politics and more. The age of the mediocrity seems to have gone by, the stale ideas have no place in the modern competitive nation which is now looking up to compete at the global level. The name of Mukesh Ambani stands out in the domain of business. You can only look with awe and wonder how this ascent could have been possible in the first place.

It is easy to say that Mukesh Ambani inherited Reliance Industries with a solid foundation laid by his father, but then, the Reliance patriarch had two sons who shared the assets almost equally, but you can compare them to conclude that one cannot rise without the qualities of head and heart, which Mukesh boosts of aplenty. What I like most about Mukesh is his adherence to the values, the ones which he has learnt from his father and mother, and those which he has inculcated himself. And these values are very simple to learn and even put in practice. While trying to find out more about him, it would be erroneous on the part of any person to know his worth, or how much he earns, or what his standing in the list of global rich is. This is the reason that, in the course of this book, we have not paid much attention to this aspect, because the fortune is transitory, and it can be made perennial only with core values and sticking to them in conjunction with hard work.

Despite his stature in the world, Mukesh has not changed much over time; you can see him dress elegantly without any flashes. When he speaks, it appears that he is a little under-confident in public, but when he makes his moves in business, he is a masterly player who has perfect command over all aspects concerning it. This command comes not from his wealth, but from the homework that he conducts before making his moves. He knows which person will suit which job, he has the uncanny ability to identify talent; and these people are leading him to success. Despite his resounding success, he remains an affectionate family member, and is keen to know the welfare of all those who are related to him. He pays diligent attention to all those people who are connected with him, whether they are his employees, shareholders or even ordinary customers. He perfectly shows that having trust and faith in the relations helps weave a solid base from which a person can spring up to success. All these values and qualities put together make him an invincible businessman. He insists to win hearts. He follows the edict that if you care for your customers, they will care for you, and this thinking of his has proved correct.

In the present scenario, hardly a day passes when there is no news about the Reliance Group: it is either about its expansion plans, or its diversification plans, or its bid for acquisition, or its tie-ups, or its plans for the consumers, or its philanthropy. The list is virtually endless, bottomless. He has raised Reliance to such a brand which you can love or hate or criticize or admire, but you can neither ignore it, nor live without it. And Mukesh's passionate leadership plays the most crucial part in this rise. I wish him good wishes for many more laurels in life.

If you ask me, what the high point of this book is, I would say that it narrates the process which has helped Mukesh Ambani and the Reliance to touch newer heights. It takes pains to reveal the background and contributing factors keeping which in sight, a decision for backward integration or diversification or expansion was taken at different times of the splendid growth story. As the Reliance strategy is analysed, explained and exemplified, the reader gets to know what is happening within the Reliance ranks, and what scripts the success story of this giant organisation headed by Mukesh Ambani. This analysis makes this book invaluable as it provides insights into the mind of the man who we look at with awe and admiration.

– A.K. Gandhi

❑

Contents

Biography

Like Father...

If success has a peculiar composition of ingredients, I suppose the life of Mukesh Ambani is the perfect example of this. To know how it works, and which spice should find how much of space, there could be no better illustration than the life of this successful business tycoon who has climbed the stairs of success without having to look back. One wonders how one could succeed unfailingly and have one's way in whatever enterprise he steps in. To know this, we would have to start not with the life of Mukesh Ambani, but that of his father–Dhirubhai Ambani, on whose foundation did he build an empire.

Dhirubhai is a perfect example of a dreamy fanciful journey from an ordinary life to an altitude where he created a niche for himself, a niche that has upped the ante for all those who seek success in life. He was not only successful, but also fortunate to have a son like Mukesh who has upped the ante still higher, so high and so elevated and so grand and so illustrious that one wonders awestruck about this mantra for success.

Dhirajlal Hirachand Ambani, better known as Dhirubhai Ambani, was born on 28 December, 1932 to Hirachand Gordhanbhai Ambani, a village schoolteacher and Jamnaben Ambani. His parents lived at Chorwad, Junagarh. These were the days of turmoil for India, as the national movement for freedom was in a full swing. Dhirubhai was a little child when he could hear the anti-British slogans being shouted in the streets in about 1939; he could hardly understand why people protested while going about, but he certainly drew joy from what he saw, he would himself gather a band of little friends and shout slogans. He seldom understood why people should protest against the British who looked more handsome and more mannered than the Indians. It was at this time that he was starting to understand how the British were atrociously suppressing Indians while they were fighting the deadly Second World War in the name of protecting democracy, freedom and human rights.

Growing up in this uncertain period, his scope of activities gradually expanded and he earned admonitions at the hands of his father. With the passage of time, the situation in the country was growing more explosive, more so in the princely state of Junagarh in which he lived. As his understanding expanded, he saw how the 1942

Quit India Movement erupted and waned, and then how Subhash Chandra Bose's name became a popular name, especially because of his adventures in the northeast. He could not understand why should Bose attack India and still find favors with the common people. By the time the ratings of the navy revolted in 1946, he had started to know what meant what to a great extent, and he himself took part in the street protests, and suffered a stick blow on his back too.

It was the time when the British found it difficult to rule India in view of the frequent protests and uprisings. The primary purpose why the British were in India was the money that they earned from this vast country; but now, it became virtually impossible for them to rule the country, as the Indians were gradually rising against them and the situation was becoming volatile. They were well aware of the potential that a united India could pose in the years to come, so they created conditions which could lead to the partition of India. Unfortunately, many leaders acted like power-hungry hounds, who accepted independence at the cost of partition. Another nail that the British thrust into India was to give the princely states an option either to join India or Pakistan or remain independent of the two.

Fortunately, India had a leader of the caliber of Sardar Patel, who integrated states. There were 562 states at that time, and he took timely steps to merge them all in the Indian union. At this time, three states posed problems – Jammu and Kashmir, Hyderabad and Junagarh, the last in which Dhirubai lived.

The princely state of Junagarh was ruled by a Muslim ruler named Nawab Muhammad Mahabat Khanji III. The population predominantly constituted the Hindus, while the rulers were Muslims, and they wished Junagarh to merge with Pakistan, which the Hindus never wanted because Pakistan was created on the basis of religion and the security of the Hindus was at stake. Already, the Hindus and the Sikhs were suffering untold miseries in the newly created territory called Pakistan. So, people in Junagarh rose in protest. And Dhirubhai joined these protests as an adolescent; he was barely 15 years now, but the cause of revolt is best served by the youth, as we have seen in the supreme sacrifices which the likes of Bhagat Singh, Chandra Shekhar Azad, Rajguru, Sukhdev, Ram Prasad Bismil, Madan Lal Dhingra and scores of others made for this country. Thankfully, Dhirubai did not have to indulge in these activities for long, because Sardar Patel was at the helm. He skillfully managed the situation and merged Junagarh into the nation body and soul after a brief police action and a plebiscite. The Nawab had no other option but to flee to Pakistan, where he settled down finally.

Now was the ripe time for Dhirubhai Ambani to settle down in life too. He and his brother, Ramnikbhai left for the Port of Aden (in Yemen) to work for A. Besse & Co. Dhirubhai was merely 16 years old when he was going to enter the wide, wide world to carve out a place for himself. Hailing from the Vaishya (business) community, the community renowned for its business acumen, he was about to prove that what is said about the community was perfectly right. He managed things such that he started to sell Shell and Burmah oil products for this company, and saw his own chances to grow. His keen power of observation stood him in good stead when he is said to have melted the silver bullion and started selling it as pure silver, because he had seen that the value of the pure silver was much higher than that of the bullion. This was only the beginning, and the time to unfold was to contain much to display his acumen and financial wizardry.

Dhirubhai was friendly and affable, he possessed an ardent desire to achieve much in his life, and with time, it transformed into a type of extreme ambition, and this cultivated in him a quality of 'risk-taking'. The life of great people is proof enough that a person can never achieve success without a measure of risk, but in his case, Dhiru was willing to go to touch the extreme.

It was at Aden in 1957 that a son was born to Dhirubai and his wife. This son, named Mukesh, was destined to shine like the Pole Star on the global horizon, but it was Dhirubhai who was working untiringly to lay the foundation on which Mukesh was destined to build his empire. Another son named Anil was born in 1959. Much in contrast, this Anil was not going to prove as lucky as his elder sibling.

In 1959, Dhirubhai took a decision to return to India in view of the frequent riots that were breaking out between the Jews and the Muslims, in which the Muslims were gaining ground, and the situation was leading to extermination of all those who belonged to different faiths. This gave Dhirubhai an opportunity to try his hand at his own business. He started 'Majin' in partnership with Champaklal Damani, his second cousin, who lived with him in Yemen. The purpose of Majin was to import polyester and export spices to Yemen.

Back in India, Dhirubai started his business by the name of Reliance Commercial Corporation. His first office was set up at the Narsinatha Street in Masjid Bunder. It was a small office, just about 33 sq m, with miniscule furniture and a telephone. He also hired two assistants to help him in his operations. It was at this time that he started to give shape to his dreams, and he knew that no person could succeed without a team at his call, so he set down to create and train a team of dedicated people who would stay with the Reliance for years to follow and take it to greater heights. The prominent names of the earliest team included Rasikbhai Meswani (his nephew), Ramnikbhai Nathubhai (his younger brother), and two former schoolmates named Rathibhai Mucchala and Narottambhai Joshi.

If the workplace was modest, the place of living for his family was equally modest; it was a two-bedroom apartment at the Jai Hind Estate located in Bhuleshwar, Mumbai.

Dhirubhai worked with a unique mindset and temperament, and not everybody liked his aptitude for risk-taking which sometimes touched the extreme limits. This proclivity on his part created a divide between him and his partner Champaklal Damani who believed in cautious treading in the business alleys and did not wish to expand into the yarn business, but Dhirubhai had seen his chances in it. The two parted ways in 1965, and the following year, Dhirubhai had his sway on the Reliance Commercial Corporation, which he later renamed as Reliance Industries on 8 May, 1973. It was at this time that he launched the brand name 'Vimal' which later became a popular brand by the name 'Only Vimal' and sold sarees, shawls, suits and other dresses. Interestingly, Vimal was the name of his elder brother Ramniklal Ambani's son. Coming to his own, a massive business tycoon was in the making now.

Right since the earliest times in his business life, Dhirubhai understood it well that there exists a close nexus between business, bureaucracy and politics. In those days of license raj, it was inevitable for a businessman to pay obeisance to create 'an atmosphere' to keep those in the power happy; and he did it too well, by assuaging the spirits of people right from the highest government official to the lowly peon. And it is well known that the politicians confer favors on the businessmen desiring to get handsome donations during election campaigns. With the rising competition in the business, it was no more sufficient to keep the leaders and bureaucrats happy, it was also essential that the competitors were kept at bay, and Dhirubhai did this well too. He had mastered the art of crushing rivals. The list of businesses in this regard is long including the Swan Mills and Kapal Mehra of Orkay; and among the bigger victims include Nusli Wadia of Bombay Dyeing and Ramnath Goenka of Indian Express. He reduced them all to a pale shadow of what they were once.

Dhirubhai worked hard to make 'Only Vimal' a common name, and he specifically targeted in the interiors of India. When people started to recognise the brand, he took the next step that was to set up retail outlets selling 'Only Vimal' textiles exclusively. As it became an established name in the market, even a technical team from the World Bank visited its manufacturing facility in 1975, and admired it.

His meteoric rise posed a challenge to the established business houses, this is what made him a target. Dhirubhai did not come from a business family, he relied more on his wits as he had no family connections to get his things done. He knew that he was bound to struggle, and overcome them; his life seemed to be one big struggle. As a businessman, Dhirubhai did not boast of ancestors who were a well-known name in the country or even state or town, this was one reason that the class-conscious businessmen did not really accept him as an equal, and this was evident when, in 1998, he was awarded the "Dean's Medal" by The Wharton School, University of Pennsylvania, the oldest business management school, and he was the first Indian to receive it. Though a number of businessmen were present, there were scores of others who abstained themselves from the function because of their 'class consciousness'. Ajay Piramal (of Piramal Group) agreed that it was strange that more of the businessmen did not turn up, "maybe they aren't happy with Ambani's great success!" But this void was made up by the presence of politicians of all hues, except of course the communists.

Dhirubhai had created a class apart for himself. He was not one of those businessmen who believed in 'swadeshi', but was the one who believed in liberalisation and globalisation, saying that he was ready to play on the front foot, and the Reliance was ready for the challenge. He did not believe in greater protection for the Indian businessmen.

Business Controversies

In the modern era, business is no more only buying and selling commodities, it involves much of common sense and making the most of opportunities. Dhirubhai did exactly this. In 1988, the Reliance Industries came up with a rights issue regarding partly convertible debentures. It added to its popularity, while it is believed that the management was making all efforts to not allow the stock prices to slide even an inch. Sensing this inclination on the part of the company, the Bear Cartel, a group of stock brokers from Calcutta, saw its chances and began to short sell the Reliance shares. As the events to unfold will show, they had picked up a wrong target.

To counter this, a group of stock brokers, until recently referred to as the 'Friends of Reliance' started to buy the short sold shares of the Reliance Industries on the Bombay Stock Exchange (BSE). The basic belief of the Bear Cartel was that the Bulls would go short of cash to complete the transactions and would be ready for settlement under the 'Badla' trading system operative in the BSE. To the astonishment of the Bear Cartel, the Bulls kept buying and a price of Rs. 152 per share was maintained until the day of settlement. The 'Friends' knew it well that the Cartel did not have the shares, so to hound them out of their wits, they gave the Bear Cartel a massive blow and demanded for physical delivery of the shares.

It is believed that much of the money was provided by Dhirubhai Ambani to the stock brokers who had bought the shares of the Reliance, to enable them to complete the transaction. In the case of non-settlement, the Bulls demanded 'Unbadla' or a penalty sum of Rs. 35 per share. With this, the demand for Reliance shares increased and they shot above Rs. 180 in minutes. This settlement caused much uproar in the market. The situation was so volatile that the BSE had to be kept closed for three business days.

To settle the matter finally, the authorities at the BSE intervened and brought down the 'Unbadla' rate to Rs. 2 per share with a stipulation that the Bear Cartel would have to make the physical delivery of the shares within the next few days. The poor Bear Cartel, it had no way out but to buy the Reliance shares from the open market at higher price levels, and it is also learnt that Dhirubhai made the most of the opportunity as he himself supplied those shares to the Bear Cartel and earned a handsome profit out of this misadventure.

The matter had been settled to the utter satisfaction of Dhirubhai Ambani, but it was natural for the questions to be raised. The main question was where from he, until recently a yarn trader and only a new industrialist, had got hold of the money enough to hold the Cartel in their tracks. This matter even found expression in the Parliament. Pranab Mukherjee, then the Union Finance Minister, answered a question that non-resident Indians had invested over Rs. 220 million in Reliance during 1982-83. These investments had also come from the companies called Crocodile, Lota and Fiasco. Further investigations by private individuals, including journalists, revealed that these companies had been registered in the Isle of Man, a tax haven and self-governing British Crown dependency located in the Irish Sea between England and Ireland, by several people all having a suffix of Shah. More questions were raised, however, the Reserve Bank of India (RBI) could find no wrongdoing in the transactions on the part of the Reliance. With this, the matter receded into oblivion.

However, it established Dhirubhai as a business tycoon. Everybody now knew that it was no easy task for anyone to meddle with him.

This entire episode also showed that it was not a mere risk, it was a well-considered move and he knew well how he could teach a lifelong lesson to the detractors; despite the fact that he was known for his risk-taking ability.

The one incident that we have described above was not the only controversy that Dhirubhai had to confront. He had also faced several other controversies, winning most of them and standing a loser to a few. It would be worthwhile to look into some of them. This will give us an insight that he had to deal with more than the normal share of jealousy and business competition wrapped in animosity; however, all these troubles did not diminish his zest for battle; he had one big dream and he was working for it that was to make the Reliance the largest private company in the country. To accomplish this ambition, he could not afford to shy away from controversies and confrontations as different events show; and he did not shy away from taking on even the finance minister and the prime minister. Let us recount a few.

Dhirubhai had an occasion to confront with V.P. Singh, both as the finance minister and prime minister. Dhirubhai knew it well that his business aspirations could not be fulfilled without the political support, so he had built up an amiable contact with Indira Gandhi. He hoped that this favor would continue on the part of the political establishment when she was assassinated on 31 October, 1984 and was succeeded by her son Rajiv Gandhi. Dhirubhai was confident that his relationship would flourish with the incumbent prime minister, but that was not to be. In the new cabinet under Rajiv Gandhi, V.P. Singh was sworn in as the Union Finance minister. He took a number of extreme steps in this capacity, which included raids against Dhirubhai Ambani and Amitabh Bachchan, among others. Many of these raids were against the pro-Congress industrialists, which irked the Congress, and he was shifted out of the ministry. V.P. Singh was powerful enough that he could not be thrown out of the cabinet, only a sideway move could be possible to tackle him, and he was made the Union Defence Minister. His stint as the Defence Minister is a memorable too, because his knowledge of the murky defence deals revealed the Bofors kickbacks, which not only brought down the Rajiv Gandhi government, but continues to hound the Congress several decades later.

Anyway, let us come back to our main topic, and see how these developments impacted Dhirubhai Ambani and the Reliance. For his manufacturing unit of polyester filament yarn, Dhirubhai needed the import of PTA (purified terephthalic acid), but as soon as V.P. Singh assumed the charge of the finance ministry, he shifted PTA from the open general license category to the limited permissible list in May 1985. Dhirubhai had got winds of this decision, so he took a pre-emptive action and tied up with a host of banks to issue letters of credit (LC) which could ensure almost a year's unhindered supply. As he had taken this action just days before the government's decision was taken, it was bound to rake up a controversy. The Finance Minister was evidently miffed at this. He immediately slapped a 50% import duty on PTA. This was how Dhirubhai came in direct confrontation with V.P.

Singh. This was bound to have impact on other matters too, which came quite too soon, indicating a tough time ahead for the Reliance.

Dhirubhai was a keen observer how finance works, and this was the reason that he virtually paid no tax. His ambition needed more funds, and it was at this time that he thought out of a new plan. He was like a god for his investors who trusted him fully. The Reliance Group had issued a great number of debentures. Dhirubhai thought that converting these debentures into equity shares would improve his company's debt equity ratio, reduce outflow on interest, and allow him to raise funds again. However, these debentures were non-convertible. He managed to convince the officers at the finance ministry about this, and the investors were too happy to accept this offer.

The trouble spot was however V.P. Singh. When he came to know of this in June 1984, the general body meeting of the Reliance was about to be held the following day; and V.P. Singh refused permission for it. The impact was felt like a massive tremor; the Reliance shares nosedived to almost half of their market value within a matter of a few hours. But as if this was not sufficient, more troubles had to follow. The public sector banks had lent to about 60 investment companies heavy amounts against the security of the Reliance shares, and these companies were now on way to buying the Reliance debentures.

Another factor that made it worse for Dhirubhai was the Indian Express. It openly alleged that these companies were the outer face of the Reliance and the whole operation could be a meaningful exercise only if the debentures were converted to shares. This allegation had an immediate after effect. The RBI set in motion, and ordered the banks to call back the loans from these companies.

It was like a massive blow to Dhirubhai personally, as his business acumen saw a big question mark. As a consequence of this upheaval, he suffered a paralytic attack in February 1986.It later came to light that the person behind the Indian Express revelations was Nusli Wadia, and this was part of the business rivalry, because both were in the competing business – Nusli Wadia was manufacturing di-methyl terephthalate, while Dhirubhai was in PTA, both of which are raw materials for manufacturing polyester yarn and fibre. At this juncture, Indian Express sided with Nusli Wadia and ran a series of stories alleging the Reliance on different scores. This volatile condition was added upon by the government when it withdrew the customs duty on PFY, which impacted the Reliance. However, Dhirubhai once again proved his mettle when a Rs. 5 billion convertible debenture issue was oversubscribed almost seven times.

Interestingly, the articles in the Indian Express were co-authored by Arun Shourie, who later as the Union Minister for Disinvestment in the Atal Behari Vajpayee government, ironically presided over the sale of 26 percent of the equity capital of the Indian Petrochemicals Corporation Ltd (IPCL) to the Reliance, which now came in the position to dominate the market for a variety of petrochemical products. In these articles, the co-author of Arun Shourie was none other than S. Gurumurthy of the Swadeshi Jagaran Manch, an affiliated organisation of the Rashtriya Swayamsevak Sangh (RSS), which is well known as the ideological basis for the BJP.

So far as V.P. Singh was concerned, he was shifted out of the finance ministry to defence. With this, the decks were cleared for Reliance; it got permission for early conversion of debentures into shares, and it also got relief in several pending matters. This was how Dhirubhai scored a victory in this case.

No fighter can win all the fights, and Dhirubhai was no exception. He indeed lost one battle in the corporate sector. That was when he vied for control over the Larsen and Toubro (L&T), which was not doing well in 1988, and Dhirubhai thought it a ripe opportunity to acquire it. The Ambani sons (Mukesh and Anil) joined the L&T board of directors, while Dhirubhai became its chairman in 1989.

At this time, Indian Express was at work raising dust storms over anything concerning the Reliance, and how then could it leave the L&T case alone? Added to it, was the support lent by V.P. Singh, who returned to the helm of affairs, now as the prime minister, for a brief but exciting tenure.

The political scene was going through a troublesome period, so far as India was concerned. The Rajiv Gandhi government was marred by a number of scandals and controversies, including the Bofors, sending of Peacekeeping Force (IPKF) to Sri Lanka, and mis-governance on the religious scene (first Ram Janmabhoomi and then Shah Bano case). The biggest critic of the government was none other than V.P. Singh. It is generally understood that he had 'inside' information on the Bofors scandal which could damage Rajiv Gandhi's reputation, but as V.P. Singh later admitted in 2005, that he had information on HDW submarine deal, and not Bofors. When he was sacked from the cabinet, he resigned from the Congress and the Lok Sabha and formed a Jan Morcha with Arun Nehru and Arif Mohammad Khan, and re-entered the Lok Sabha from Allahabad (now Prayagraj). It was like a meteoric rise for him.

V.P. Singh fought the general elections in 1989, as the leader of the National Front, headed by him, in understanding with the Bharatiya Janata Party (BJP) and the Left parties, and succeeded to secure a simple majority. The BJP and the Left parties declined to join the government and agreed to support the government from outside.

Even before the government could be sworn in, it was confronted with a controversy. V.P. Singh had entered the electoral fray as a clear PM candidate against Rajiv Gandhi, but when a meeting was held, on 1 December, 1989, to choose a leader for the post, V.P. Singh proposed the name of Devi Lal, a Jat leader from Haryana, but he declined the offer, and proposed the name of V.P. Singh. Chandra Shekhar saw a rotten rat in it, as he himself saw a probable candidate for the high post. He refused to even take part in the cabinet.

Anyway, this made V.P. Singh the next prime minister, he was sworn in the next day, 2 December, 1989. He served as the PM for a little less than a year, but that never means his term was without excitement. He first touched the Mandal Commission report, which brought turmoil in the country. When he found that the Dhirubhai Ambani had taken over as the chairman of the L&T, his old wounds swelled again, and V.P. Singh acted through the government-owned financial institutions like the Life Insurance Corporation of India (LIC) and General Insurance Corporation of India (GIC) to stonewall the takeover. Dhirubhai sensed defeat and resigned from the board of directors.

I suppose I should also narrate how V.P. Singh was voted out of power. He ordered the arrest of Lal Krishna Advani when his Rathyatra reached Samastipur on way to Ayodhya. This prompted the BJP to withdraw the support, and in the ensuing trust vote, his government was voted out of power 142-346. This gave Chandra Shekhar an opportunity to see his chance and he was sworn in as the next PM on the Congress outside support. Even his government lasted a few months. It was really a period of instability and uncertainty for India.

Even long after his stint as PM, V.P. Singh never seemed to have forgotten his animosity against the Reliance. In 2006, after he had made a bid to revive his Jan Morcha, he proceeded to Dadri to join the farmers agitating against the acquisition of land by the Reliance Industries, owned by Anil Ambani, and demanding adequate compensation. Singh was arrested. He made more than one attempt for this, and once succeeded to evade the police and join the farmers too.

Coming back to the L&T controversy, Reliance sold its holdings to the Grasim, and even this transaction attracted criticism as the Securities and Exchange Board of India (SEBI) pointed out that the Reliance should not have bought L&T shares a few months prior to deciding to sell its shares, and for this, the Reliance was also made to pay a fine.

Another controversy that made Dhirubhai look below the mark was that of the share switch. This pertained to the incident when the Unit Trust of India (UTI) sent some Reliance shares to its registrars for transfer, but it received back some other shares, with different numbers. This started the rumours that something was fishy about this, to the extent of fake shares in the market. An investigation was launched by SEBI, but it did not find any evidence, though it pointed out a number of discrepancies in numbering and transferring shares. As a result of this, SEBI ordered the Reliance Consultancy Services (the Reliance registrars) to shut shop. This saved the face for the Reliance to some extent, but then, another controversy was waiting to come into being.

When the telecom sector was opened up initially, a clear demarcation was made between basic and cellular operators. The Reliance acquired basic licenses in several telecom sectors. About this time, WiLL (wireless in local loop) technology allowed the basic operators a feasibility of some mobility. The idea was revolutionary; however, it was not to the liking of the cellular operators, as they described it as an infringement on their licenses, which they had paid for heftily. Moreover, this brought the Reliance critics to cry hoarse as Reliance was expected to gain much from the WiLL at the cost of the cellular operators.

The Telecom Regulator Authority of India (TRAI), however, allowed limited mobility to basic operators, with a number of restrictions in force. The parties took to a legal battle, but ever since the technological landscape has undergone a complete change.

These are not the only controversies against Dhirubhai. He was also accused of 'buying peace' with the income tax officials. He was on several occasions accused of manipulating balance sheets and other accounts. Even some of his executives have been found involved in controversies; for example, two of them were accused of violating the Official Secrets Act after a cabinet note was found in their possession during a police raid. Further, one of these officials was allegedly linked to a mafia don.

It has also been said that he maintained an office on the outskirts of Delhi. It was staffed by the retired bureaucrats, and their main assignment was to keep tabs on their former colleagues. They were mainly assigned to create a favorable environment for the Reliance with different ministries, and various measures were undertaken for this purpose. These people also kept information on the children of senior bureaucrats so that they could be sent abroad for higher studies. Similarly, on Diwali, the biggest gift-giving occasion in the country, boxes of candies were sent out to different staff members of ministries, and each box is said to have a gold or silver piece inside. The time has shown that these practices have kept the Reliance in the good books and they were able to get prior information about the decisions-to-be-taken.

Height of Popularity

Did only business make Dhirubhai Ambani a household name? Perhaps not entirely, more things worked to make him so. Rather, he indulged in things not strictly business if seen in isolation, but surely business if seen from the height of success that he attained.

He was well aware of the making and unmaking of the political parties. He had seen parties gaining and losing popular favor at the hustings, so he discriminated little when he showered favors on leaders of different political hues; that was to make sure that he was sure to remain in favor whatever the party ascended the power. And this was the reason that the Reliance was humorously termed as the most powerful political party in India. This is the reason that few political leaders possessed the gumption to oppose him or his heirs for that matter. He also showered favors on the media, so few of them chose to go against him or his establishment. And the ones which chose to go against him, they were bound to face troubles, as we have cited cases to show. So was the case with the bureaucrats.

Above all, Dhirubhai cared for his shareholders. He rewarded them handsomely not only in monetary terms, but also in adulatory terms. He called them family members. These gestures convinced the middle class to invest in the Reliance. He was known for his meddling with the share prices and admitted to 'thin and circular trading' for the purpose.

In expansion of his business, he adopted a unique approach. While most businessmen favor to borrow from financial institutions, Dhirubhai raised money from the public at large to fund his large industrial ventures. He paid more attention to the investors in small towns, rather than those of big cities; and to make his presence felt, he opened his Vimal stores there and promoted his brand. Even he himself did not shy away from inaugurating the franchise outlets himself, often several of them on the same day.

When his supporters were asked about the controversies concerning Dhirubhai, they would simply say that there is no businessman, big or small, in India who is not accused of these manipulations; in fact, manipulations are part of the business. Even he himself once acknowledged to the Time magazine that he was no Mother Teresa. Perhaps Manas Chakravarty has described him in most perfect words as "...it was (Dhirubhai's) common touch combined with his uncommon vision that was the secret of his success."

Dhirubhai supported not only his shareholders, but also his workers. He has often gone out of the way to help them. It is popularly said about him that he was present whenever any of his team members was facing a difficulty, as if he were a god, as if he knew by the magic wand what was happening where.

If Dhirubhai supported his workers, they too, in turn, never failed him. They have displayed their competence on several occasions. It was his faith in his team members that achieved to build the petroleum refinery at Jamnagar in three years at a capital cost that was 30 percent lower than other comparable projects. It was his cherished team that succeeded to restart the Patalganga project within one month of the sudden floods in July 1989. This is the faith of both shareholders and team members which has helped the Reliance to soar high in the infinite sky.

Dhirubhai also believed in charity, but he never propagated it. Often, the beneficiary did not know who had helped him in fact. His inspiring words were to 'dream big with open eyes,' 'limitations were only in the mind' and 'no is no answer.' He was the man who displayed his qualities all the time, constantly; he never seemed under-confident and doubtful about his own talent, and little was he doubtful about the talent that his team members possessed. A mix of all these traits made him the man we know him to be.

Dhirajlal Hirachand, better known as Dhirubhai Ambani, had suffered a paralytic stroke in 1986. In 2002, he suffered a massive stroke again. He was admitted to the Breach Candy Hospital in Mumbai, where he remained in coma for a week before he breathed his last on 6 July, 2002. This put an end to the illustrious life of enterprise, but the lamp he lighted continues to glow so brightly and splendidly that all other lamps seem to lose their glory in its bright shine. He achieved what others could simply call impossible. He built India's largest privately controlled business empire from a scratch, he possessed merely Rs. 50,000 when he returned from Aden. He had traversed an upright path from Aden where he had started as a mere gas attendant; and wonder, he would rise to be the chairman of the company that owned India's largest and world's fifth largest oil refinery. A man had passed away who called success his biggest enemy. But his popularity did not rest only on his success; his cremation was attended by well-heeled people as well as ordinary people, together making a throng unseen before. His ease of communication with the rich as well as the poor made him a man you could either love or hate but couldn't be indifferent to. His personality encompassed many facets. He was a visionary who knew what he wanted, and he was a manipulator as well who knew how he could get his things done.

At the time of his death, the Reliance group of companies, led by Dhirubhai Ambani, had a gross annual turnover of Rs. 75,000 crore (or US $ 15 billion). Compare this with the annual turnover of Rs. 70 crore in 1975-76, and Rs. 3,000 crore in 1990-91. At this time, the Reliance was in diverse fields including synthetic fibers, textiles and petrochemical products, oil and gas exploration, petroleum refining, telecommunications and financial services.

In his lifetime, Dhirubhai often wondered at the success that he had achieved, and why not thousands of others flourish as he did, only they would need to dream big as he did. He also wondered the kind of economic power India could become if all these entrepreneurs succeeded to achieve their ambitions.

Years before his death, Dhirubhai said, "Dhirubhai will go one day. But Reliance's employees and shareholders will keep it afloat. Reliance is now a concept in which the Ambanis have become irrelevant."

He was conferred a number of awards in his lifetime. The highest award was the Padma Vibhushan which was conferred posthumously. A number of books have been written on him. A Hindi film, Guru, directed by Mani Ratnam, is said to be inspired by the life of Dhirubhai depicting how a budding man goes on to create a niche for himself in the cut-throat business world. Atal Behari Vajpayee paid rich tributes to him. He stated, "The country has lost iconic proof of what an ordinary Indian fired by the spirit of enterprise and driven by determination can achieve in his own lifetime."

How Mukesh Ambani Feels About His Father

On different occasions, Mukesh has described the massive impression that he and his siblings got under the towering personality of the patriarch. In fact, this aspect of his life will keep coming during the course of this book. In an interview with Pritish Nandy, Mukesh Ambani has revealed several anecdotes about his father. He says that he was 'always very responsible and enterprising'. The world knows that Dhirubhai started work as an attendant at a gas station, but in fact, he had earned money even before that when he opened his own shop at Chorwad, a small town in Junagarh, to sell bhajia to pilgrims over the weekend. He also reveals that he wore only pants until he set out for Aden.

From his childhood, Dhirubhai was very enterprising and adventurous. Mukesh says that this spirit was in him right since childhood, and this was what took him to Aden, which was no paradise or promised something great, but he wanted to feel adventure in the wide, wide world. So far as education is concerned, he was only an SSCL pass, that too he passed it in his second attempt. Mukesh smiles when he says that 'it was like MABF'. That simply means Matric Appeared But Failed.

According to Mukesh, his father started work at the petrol pump, and then moved to logistics, loading the ships and airplanes, and ensured that everything turned out smoothly. Speaking about the spirit of adventure, Mukesh recalls an anecdote. Let us listen it in his own words: "Once they were on a ship, attending a party. From the ship to the shore was more than a kilometre. Some people at the party were betting among themselves–that whoever could jump into the cold water and swim to the shore would get an ice cream. It was a joke and no one took it seriously. Papa heard it and turned around and asked them: Is that a deal? Everyone thought he was kidding.

But he took off his shirt and jumped into the water and actually swam all the way to the shore. That was the kind of person he was."

Mukesh reveals that his father had gone to Aden to earn some handsome money, and he returned from there with Rs. 50,000 in his pocket. It might seem to be a small sum these days, but in those days, it was a 'pretty neat kitty', as he wanted to do his own business. Taking cues from the first employers, Pedhi, Dhirubhai entered the textile business, but he was a visionary, and saw where the future of the sector lay. He wanted to do something for the future of the textiles. It was about this time that polyester had been launched, and in it, he saw his chance. He had not chosen polyester because he felt like, rather he had studied it well and compared it with fibres, and it was only then that he betted for it. By the mid-sixties, he rose to be the largest polyester trader at the time when they did not have a plant for it. His vision proved right, over time it took over 70 percent of the market share.

Mukesh admits that the Reliance has been built on the pillars of polyester. Today, the Reliance is one of the biggest in polyester in the world. He also says that his father decided to diversify into petrochemicals 'primarily to feed the polyester industry' and then they went on to further expand into plastics, refineries, oil, gas and finally telecommunication. Mukesh earnestly states: "We have a whole host of infrastructure portfolios today, but it all began with Papa's vision for polyester. It was the lifeline for Reliance."

Mukesh also remembered his grandfather and wished that he lived to see what they achieved in the years to follow, but his grandmother had seen much of the success story which unfolded until 1979.

When Pritish Nandy pointed out that Dhirubhai was not known for his humility, but for his impatience, Mukesh stated that they called it 'infectious impatience', and he went on to add that they are trying to inculcate this spirit in the entire organisation. He defined 'infectious impatience' as not only to get things done, but also to 'get it done in double quick time'. Describing the biggest achievement of his father, Mukesh said that it was building morale, because he valued it most and he was master at motivating people. Not only this, the Reliance had about 4-5 million people as shareholders, but Dhirubhai wanted to expand it to 40-50 million, or even bigger to 500 million.

Speaking about his parents, Anil Ambani said that when they lived in the backstreets of Mumbai, in a chawl at Kabootarkhana, a cooperative society inhabited by about 600 families, each sharing a single bedroom accommodation, "...people find it shocking that neither I nor Mukesh drink or smoke, are vegetarian, are god fearing and don't gamble". These were the kind of values that Dhirubhai and his wife inculcated in the children. Anil further states: "These are not values that are passed on by any sort of action, but more a part of one's upbringing. Praying to God, respecting other individuals...I think it's been really put together by my mother." Anil also claims clear memories of living in the chawl. They were seven family members and had to make do in the one-room apartment; and one hundred families had to share a common bathroom and toilet in the chawl. He also remembers that his apartment was located on the fourth floor, needing to climb about 50-60 steps.

Values are inculcated the hard way, Anil recalls. By the time the family moved to Usha Kiran accommodation, they were facing no lack of financial resources, yet Dhirubhai allowed the children only goal-oriented finances. He often asked children to earn their pocket money. For example, after an outdoor activity, like hiking or trekking or game, he would give children an offer to have one snack and a drink, or two snacks but no drink. The budget for this was just five rupees and this amount stood for a long time.

Dhirubhai had a uni-dimensional focus on the Reliance, as if his life could not thrive outside his venture. His passion and focus made him very busy, yet he was for his family on Sundays. Whatever be the pressures of his work, the Sundays were for the kids. This is the thing he taught his children too. On other days, he found it hard to give them even a minute, but he made up for this deficiency in a novel way. He issued an advertisement in the newspaper asking for the services of a non-academic teacher as a home tutor. Non-academic in the sense that the tutor was not supposed to help the kids in education, rather he was to help them grow and develop. He interviewed a number of teachers before finally selecting Mahendrabhai Vyas. This teacher came and stayed with the kids in the evening, and did hordes of activities including games, conversation, stories and what not. Mukesh recalls that he was an important factor in their mental development. Dhirubhai never visited the kids' school; he left his kids alone when it came to education; he wanted them to choose what they wanted to study, which school they wanted to go to. This was the reason that Mukesh went for a BE degree in chemical engineering.

On Sundays, when Dhirubhai was at home, he preferred to undertake activities which were normally outside the ordinary realm of education and nutrition, which most other people do. Mukesh gives credit to his father for the love that the kids have developed for nature and wildlife. He recalls that his father used to take them out to different places, including for a walk through the forests and for a bath in the streams. This kind of upbringing has helped the children to grow into adorable personalities.

Anil also recalls an interesting anecdote, which was quoted by Vir Sanghvi in the rediff.com as an extract of his interview with Anil Ambani. He narrates in these words: "I recall it was the summer of 1970s and he (Dhirubhai) said to us, 'Look this is the mango season, I know you guys are very fond of mangoes, but the only way you can get a full box of mangoes is if you travel by the lower deck on the Bombay to Goa steamer.' And you know, our incentive was the mangoes, and not the trip to Goa." Anil further states that his father could have easily sent them to Goa by air, but he wanted us to go through that 'lower deck experience' where there was no reservation and everybody was puking; he did this because he felt there was no way the children could buy that sort of experience anywhere and at any point of time in life.

Dhirubhai was very particular about inculcation of values in his children. When the children were sent to far-off places for higher studies, the mother was apprehensive, but Dhirubhai wanted them to have that experience. The mother was afraid that her vegetarian children, with little practical experience about the external world, would die of starvation, but Dhirubhai would say that the campus experience would help them develop their personality, it would be an invaluable experience of a lifetime. He was of the view that experience cannot be measured in terms of money, it is bottomless in terms of value. Anil recalls that conditions helped to learn how to cook, how to clean up, how to iron his clothes, how to clean his toilet, and many other chores, and all these added up to the confidence building which is sure to make life meaningful.

Anil Ambani revealed the antecedents of his mother in these words: "My mother is a very simple down-to-earth person. My grandfather, that's my mother's father, was a postman. He rose to become the in-charge of a post office in Jamnagar in Gujarat. So she comes from that background."

Anil Ambani also recalls that he found his father very busy; he rarely spent time with the children, or sat with the children's homework, or anything of the sort. Children's education and upbringing were totally delegated to the mother who was a high school, and did not understand much of what the children were studying. Anil recalls to have asked his father what he missed most in life, and every time he was asked this question, he would say that he missed education. Dhirubhai wanted to study, but didn't have the resources. This was the reason that he did not want his children to have any such lack when it came to education.

The website rediff.com has quoted him narrating this experience in these words: "My father looked at it very simply, saying 'I think we are going to give you the best upbringing to help create the best values for you. I believe you have the brains, so you study hard. You don't have the financial problems that I had when I wanted to study. Well you don't have any monetary problems, so go and try to look for the best school, college, university that you can go to'."

Dhirubhai had clear ideas about the working stage of life. He believed that youth is the age to work, and every single day was precious in life. Anil Ambani recalls that when he completed his masters at Wharton in 14 months, which he was supposed to do in 24 months, and flew back home, he was damn sure that his father was going to allow him a few days break, if not a few weeks. He wanted to chill out in this time. But his father bluntly refused him a break. He said, "Absolutely not. You are going this evening to Ahmedabad and that's where you will stay for the next few years and look after our textile business." When Anil protested desiring to have a break, pet came the reply, "There will be enough time in the future to enjoy life, this is the time for you to work." And then there was no more question or argument, he had to catch the evening flight to his next post, Ahmedabad, where he stayed for the next five-six years, where he worked five days a week.

Dhirubhai has an inspiring message for the budding youths. He says that working from the shop floor, all the way to the top, was the right way to do it. However, he was very critical of the young MBA graduates, whom he described as those who thought they knew it all. With their MBA degrees in their pocket, they try to overawe even the experienced workers. This inclination caused a trouble to Mukesh and Anil Ambani in the period after Dhirubhai suffered a paralytic attack. Within the company there were several factions which they had to deal with.

How you can get respect from others, Dhirubhai has clear cut notions. He classifies the bosses into two categories: one those who command respect and second those who demand respect. He advised his children that they could develop the ability either to command respect or to demand respect. If you are in a commanding mode, people will respect you for what you are, and if you are in a demanding mode, people won't respect you, and rather they will say all sort of things when you turn your back to them.

❑

...Like Son

Stepping into his father's shoes, Mukesh Ambani has displayed that he truly deserves to be the heir to the great Dhirubhai Ambani. Mukesh has not only preserved what he inherited, but has taken it forward with added glory, helping the Reliance to shine on the global horizon. Like his father, Mukesh believes that economic realism has finally arrived in India, and if India has any future, it lies in only its becoming an economic power. If India wishes to dominate the world, this power can come only from people who can cope with economic realism, and it is the goal towards which India must work. That alone will reserve its place among the mighty nations of the world. In his economic realism, Mukesh does not lose sight of millions of Indians who should be the focus of the thought process, because the country can be on the right track if their welfare, their future and their opportunities for self-realization are on the right track. India cannot survive and flourish without the common man's welfare being looked for. India can grow, flourish and prosper when its citizens too grow, flourish and prosper. In fact, the common man is like the nerve centre, the axle of the vehicle, who can drive the economy with his purchasing power, which can be attained only through his prosperity and growth.

Mukesh Ambani was born on 19 April, 1957 at Aden, then a British colony, and now a part of Yemen where his father had started his career. His father is the legendary business tycoon Dhirubhai Ambani and his mother is Kokilaben Ambani. Mukesh was not yet one year old when his father decided to return to India and begin his own business. Mukesh also has a younger brother Anil Ambani and two sisters Nina Bhadrashyam and Dipti Dattaraj Salgaocar.

Upon returning to India, his father entered business of spices and textiles, but it was textiles to which he paid more attention, and named his business 'Vimal' after the name of his nephew, and later he changed this brand name to 'Only Vimal'. It was the beginning of the business, and the entire family lived in a chawl, a communal colony, and managed to have only a two-room apartment in Bhuleshwar, Mumbai, and this went on until 1970s. As the business was in the process of seeing brighter days ahead, his father had to make do with public transport for travel and a small office with barely any furniture.

With rising prosperity, Dhirubhai paid attention to the education of his wards. Mukesh attended the Hill Grange High School at Peddar Road. Here he was joined by his brother Anil and Anand Jain, who was to later become his close associate. Having passed his secondary examination here, he moved on to join the St. Xavier's College and then joined the Institute of Chemical Technology to obtain a B.E. degree in chemical engineering. This degree gave him a keen understanding how his father's business in polyester could be transformed into a large venture. At this time, his father's business was still a small, but fast growing enterprise.

Mukesh says that upbringing has a great impact on life. He says that the attitude and ambition that he nurtured during the course of his upbringing at home continue to stay with him, and years later when he was bringing up his own children, he realizes how difficult it must have been for his father to cultivate those qualities and thinking in them, because he finds them tough when he, as a parent, tries to cultivate these qualities in his children.

Mukesh also admits that there are benefits of being the eldest child in the family, though the parents may not, and often do not, differentiate between the children. He recalls that within the family, they had to live within the broad boundaries specified by the family, and often these boundaries were revealed when a particular incident occurred; however, within those boundaries, the children were not micro-managed. He also recalls that he interfered in the life of his children: Isha, Akash and Anant more than his father did, and admits that he might be a more anxious parent than his father could have been.

A child can find his best potential when he is allowed freedom to a reasonable degree, and this is what Mukesh got in his childhood. He remembers that his father never visited his school. Nonetheless, he was interested in his all-round development for which he did amazing things, like he employed a home tutor for the children, and he selected this teacher from amongst many through a long-drawn process of interviews, and finally selected Mahendrabhai Vyas. What is more interesting to know is that this tutor was not supposed to help children in their education; his responsibility was completely non-academic. The tutor visited them in the evening and stayed with the children up to 6.30-7. His job was to oversee how we grew. He told the children tales, played with them, built their general knowledge and gave them a bit of his mind how he saw things around him.

Mukesh also recalls that during their childhood, they did several activities including playing games, watching matches, travelling in buses and trains, and exploring different parts of Bombay. They also went camping and staying in a village for 10-15 days each year.

In this way, Dhirubhai was making up for his lack of time which he could devote to his family. This also helped the children to learn more varied things in life and develop diverse tastes. If the children became interested in wildlife or arts or culture, this kind of upbringing was responsible to a great extent. And the fun was that the children never realized that they were being taught, so subtle the learning was.

Mukesh also recalls that his father shared his passion for business and entrepreneurship from early on. This was the reason that Mukesh attended office from the earliest days of school. He admits that most of his learning comprises what he learnt from education in which his father little interfered, from Mahendrabhai, from his father's passion and from the deep feelings that his father had for the family. Mukesh also admits that all these virtues and values have stayed with him and his brother and sister all these years, perhaps they are the common bond that he shares with his siblings.

When Mukesh opted for chemical engineering, it surprised many, because at that time, Vimal was already a successful brand, and everybody hoped that he would go for textile engineering. Mukesh was first selected for an undergraduate degree in IIT Kanpur, but when the Inter-science results were announced a few days later, he joined the University Department of Chemical Technology (UDCT) along with his friends. Mukesh says that he went for chemical engineering because it promised a future for the Reliance. In an interview, Mukesh laughs, "Think of the line from the movie The Graduate, which was popular in our times: 'There is a great future in plastics.' Perhaps this left a mark on my mind." Becoming serious, he said that it was certainly in tune with the tenets on which his father built the Reliance: always invest in businesses of the future and invest in talent. He feels proud of this clear notion and says that he continues to follow these tenets even today.

Even during his college years, Mukesh was working for the Reliance almost full time. After the college was over at 2.30 pm, he would straight go to office and contribute in his father's passion whatever he could. One day, when his father was away to the US, a government agency conducted a raid; and just imagine the situation, a 17-year-old youth tackled the situation all by himself.

After his engineering degree, Mukesh joined his several friends to write several competitive examinations, as the youths are wont to do at this stage of life. This action on part of a youth is driven by the desire to prove himself, no different was the case with Mukesh. He also appeared for the civil services examination just to see if he can get into the merit list. And then as a change of mind, he started to apply to business schools for higher studies, and he was selected for the top 2-3 business schools, and chose Stanford for himself.

Mukesh sailed abroad to join the Stanford University for an MBA degree, but his father felt that real-life skills were harnessed through harsh realities and experiences of life, and not by sitting in the classroom and asked Mukesh to return and join him in the business. Mukesh abandoned his degree programme midway and returned to India. Reliance had been granted the license to manufacture, and his father wanted him to return immediately, though Mukesh was keen on completing his graduation at Stanford and also undergo the World Bank's Young Professional Programme (YPP), which was considered very prestigious in those days. But Dhirubhai wanted to put his elder son in business immediately. Mukesh even suggested that they could wait for one year and a half to start the polyester plant, but Dhirubhai wanted to start it immediately. That was how Mukesh flew back and was at work in no time. Ironically, in a recent interview, Mukesh said that today's MBA has only a snob value and is not rooted in reality.

Upon his return, Dhirubhai put him in command of a yarn manufacturing project in his company. Mukesh returned like an obedient son, and also proved that his faith in his father's command was worthy. He also remembered the teachers who influenced him much. He especially remembered the names of William F. Sharpe and Man Mohan Sharma. In his own words, they are the kind of professors 'who make you think out of the box'.

With his return in 1981, Mukesh was put under the charge of Rasikbhai Meswani, who became his first boss. Mukesh had worked in the Reliance as a school student, and knew much about how the company functioned. Rasikbhai, in particular, followed an open management style, in which one could walk into another's office and even take part in the meetings. But so far as Mukesh was concerned, this style of open management did not last long, as his father wished that he needed to be put under a boss to learn the company's ethos.

It was under Rasikbhai's charge that Mukesh learnt on-job work; he oversaw different operations such as importing polyester fibre, texturising it and selling it to textile mills. This business was quite different from the previous textile mill that they had at Naroda (Ahmedabad). His education in chemical engineering and management also helped him in this business, as he was able to organise the work better, created a heterogeneous reporting structure in the company and put into practice the newer ideas of how to motivate people. While undertaking streaks of innovation in these fields, he realized that he lagged behind his father and Rasikbhai greatly. Under these two stalwarts, Mukesh learnt much and feels grateful. He said once that the working style was like a partnership, and he was made to contribute from the day one. He also feels that he was able to learn because of the guidance and supervision of the two great people, and would also like the young people to learn in the organisation much like he did in his initial years in business. He feels that it is essential to give leverage to the young people to contribute with novel ideas, rather than to discard them outright.

It is the college time when some of your habits start to be founded. He found taste in traditional food, and grew special liking for South Indian cuisines, especially idli and sambar. He is a frequent visitor to Mysore Café, a popular café in Central Mumbai, dating back to 1930s. He is also fond of chapattis made from Bajra (a coarse grain). His wife Nita says that the greatest thing about Mukesh is that he likes to live very simple; and his vision is not limited to only the Reliance, it is for the whole of the nation. He is a born optimist. He has remained a vegetarian and is a teetotaler. He is keen to keep his good health, and finds Yoga a powerful medium to do it. Once he had remarked that Yoga is like an eternal light, which if lit once in life continues to glow and its glory never fades. The kind of status he has achieved for himself, he has to pass through tense moments regularly; it is at such junctions that he finds Yoga as a vigorous means to sustain himself and keep his nerves in check. This helps him to focus himself on the goals he has set for himself. He likes to keep himself updated on any developments taking place around him including technology, sports and entertainment. And of course, business is in his blood.

In 1981, Mukesh was in his family business body and soul. The Reliance Industries Ltd. had already expanded into newer sectors of refining and petrochemicals. The latter was specifically added in order to get a source of raw material for the polyester manufacturing. Besides, the business also included products and services in retail and telecommunications.

As Mukesh gained experience in the business, under the watchful eyes of his father, who allowed him freedom to take independent decisions, and also allowed him to take risks. This laid the foundation for a businessman who was to shine on the world horizon like the Pole Star. If an account of his rise is taken into account, it becomes a fat ledger, even this would not be enough to record all his achievements. His standing in the world is in upward trajectory continuously, week after week. Any statement about his standing at any one time proves the writer wrong, because by the time it goes into print, he has another achievement up his sleeve; he is rising so quickly. For example, while I write this sentence, the news has poured in that Mukesh Ambani has eclipsed the richest European, France's Bernard Arnault, to become the world's fourth richest person, with his wealth standing at $80.6 billion. By the time I finish this book, I am sure that he would have ascended higher, though there remain only a few steps ahead of him, and then he would have to set his own standards.

License Raj

When Mukesh became active in his family business, the country was going through an era, better known as 'license raj'. The system of license raj put several restrictions before businessmen. After independence in 1947, the country was facing numerous problems; of these the two were lack of infrastructure and unemployment. Lack of infrastructure meant that facilities were absent on the basis of which further development could take place, and so the Five Year Plans were planned. (Let us not forget that 1962 debacle was primarily due to lack of infrastructure of border roads.) Unemployment meant that people had no jobs and consequently no income, so they could not spend on goods which could set the economy in motion. To tackle these problems, the government decided to have a planned economy. This idea was rooted in the thinking that the government should take lead in the production of goods, so public sector industries were set up. And in case a private individual wished to set up an industry, he would have to seek approval from numerous government agencies (which numbered as many as 80!). Seeking approvals from so many different agencies meant wastage of a lot of time and energy, and you know, how a government files moves. Jokingly it is said that anything will lose its speed if a weight is kept on it, but just the reverse is the case when it comes to a government file; it moves swiftly when it has a weight (bribery) on it. So, the entire system was rooted in corruption. And the story doesn't end here. Even after a license was granted, the obstacles did not vanish as further licenses were needed. The government regulated the quantity of goods produced, the capital used and the sale prices; all these proved major hurdles for any businessman and inefficiencies seeped in the business. The government interference continued throughout its life not only in operation, but also in administration, as the government had the power to prevent companies from laying off workers or closing down factories. This simply meant that a businessman would have to endure a loss and yet continue with it.

The system of license raj also had its adverse impact on the imports. The import of manufactured goods from other countries was subjected to very high tariffs and foreign manufacturers needed licenses to sell their goods in India. This discouraged the foreign investors. This led to smuggling of goods, even that of everyday items. I remember a friend who smuggled in two dozen toothbrushes from Singapore for his family. Despite all the curbs, small vendors thrived which sold genuine or fake foreign goods in the streets in metros.

All this system led to setting up of public sector industries, which gave jobs to people, the jobs which were secure. The security of a job made workers believe that they couldn't be fired even if they were inefficient. These workers when pressurized often started hartals and strikes, and threatened the management; and this brought in inefficiency. This turned numerous public sector industries into 'white elephants.' Only a few made profits, and even they did not function at their full capacities, leave alone expansio'n. This system had started by Nehru, despite objections from several leaders including Dr. Ambedkar and C. Rajagopalachari. These leaders rejected this idea saying that the economic system of the country should better be left alone to adjust to the changing demands of the people and the government should not unnecessarily interfere in it. C. Rajagopalachari, the founder of the Swatantra Party, was a votary of free economy, and described the Indian model of socialism as 'Quota-Permit-License Raj'.

The license raj system, as chosen by India, was a middle path between the extremes of free economy (like that of America) and closed economy (like those of USSR, China), with myriad checks on prices and quantities to achieve a 'socialist pattern of society'. This system was also known as 'mixed economy'. With time, newer sectors of the economy were brought under the license raj. In all these sectors, it was a difficult proposition for any private company to survive. This system was thought good for the economy, but if you look at the data of the world's comparable economies, like those of Pakistan, South Korea and Indonesia, you will find that they all were doing better in terms of growth of industrial production and GDP; we were lagging behind even Pakistan, as we are often wont to compare ourselves with it. Nehru believed that this economic system would work wonders with the economy, but just the opposite had happened. So, a change in thinking began to dawn from 1980s that the system of license raj needed a change. This thinking had arisen from the belief that India had been dealing with the economy with a little too heavy hand, and this approach was stifling the economic growth and was preventing the economy from reaching its full potential. This makeover could not be achieved without having to abolish the license raj system. Voices began to be heard against it, and this was sure to have its impact in the days to follow. The concrete change in the license raj started to come about from the 1990s, but the Ambanis had been in business before the economy was put in the process of deregulation. And they had to face all these challenges which were by no means small.

When Mukesh entered business in 1981, his father had already made Reliance a name to reckon with. It was also the time that the Indira Gandhi government decided to open PFY (polyester filament yarn) manufacturing to the private sector also, yet no respite was given in the license raj system. Now, Reliance decided to apply for the license, and was supposed to tackle both of the government machinery and the competition. The license raj was known to favor you know whom, and the Reliance was a novice in the manufacturing field, while those in competition included the already established names such as those of Tatas and Birlas and 43 others, and with such stalwarts in race, there was little chance for the Reliance to succeed in the endeavour. To the astonishment of everybody concerned, Reliance was granted the license. As we have narrated in the previous section of this book, this achievement was that of Dhirubhai.

Dhirubhai also saw this as a chance to introduce Mukesh into the business. He believed that real-life experiences would make Mukesh a better businessman that he could expect to become with the MBA degree in his pocket. Dhirubhai entrusted Mukesh with the building up of the PFY plant. It was like the first major challenge for the budding youth, but he did it successfully.

In the company, Mukesh was put under the charge of Rasikbhai Meswani, then the executive director, to whom he reported daily. The company was being built from the scratch, and Mukesh was given a free hand even though he had little experience. The basic principle on which Mukesh worked in the company was that everybody ought to contribute in the plant, and this contribution was not limited to only a select few people. When such a spirit prevails in any organisation, everybody feels related to it. So was the case in this enterprise. The plant came into operation successfully. This principle was going to stay with the company in its future expansion, in which every worker, high or low, was made to feel that he was something in the company and that the system allowed him to voice his concerns. One of my friends in the company says that he had hopped out of three companies over a short duration of four years, and ever since he joined the Reliance three decades ago, he has continued to stick with it, and will retire from it when the company allows it. This is the kind of affinity the company builds for its employees.

Seeking to obtain everybody's contribution proved a bedrock for the company, especially after the death of Rasikbhai Meswani in 1985 and after his father suffered a paralytic attack in 1986, when Mukesh was required to take up responsibility head on. Of course, Dhirubhai continued to oversee the company operations right until his death in 2002.

Mukesh enjoyed the business and he had no more thought of joining back his university programme at Stanford. He was now body and soul in Reliance, and earnestly worked for its expansion and diversification. He was growing in an atmosphere where his father often said, "If you don't build your dream, someone else will hire you to help them build theirs." And in his case, he need not build his dream from the very scratch, a sturdy foundation was already present over which he needed to erect his monument of success.

Mukesh played a lead role in venturing into a vast array of areas including communications, infrastructure, petrochemicals, petroleum refining, polyester fibres, and gas and oil production. He has created several new world class manufacturing facilities involving diverse technologies that have raised Reliance's petrochemicals manufacturing capacities from less than a million tonnes to above fourteen million tonnes per annum. He has already planned to expand these capacities to double to twenty-seven million tonnes in not a long period of time.

Under the supervision of his father, Mukesh realized that it was necessary to have command over diverse factors in order to be successful, which mainly included a deep knowledge of the environment in which he worked, the massive technical and technological innovations that were taking place in the world, the newer challenges faced in marketing, training for project execution skills – all of these together without forgetting the most essential factor of the human resources. While it was necessary to pay attention to training and motivation of the workers, it was equally compulsory to keep all 'friends' in good humour. His father had already made his tactics known to the world to the extent that rules in the government could be bent at one's convenience, the fact being how far one was ready to go for that purpose.

Mukesh was learning these tactics keenly as they will stand in good stead for him in the days to come.

If this narration sounds unethical to you in some measure, let us tell you that these tactics had been in operation by a number of traditional business families; only Dhirubhai had excelled in these. Once Dhirubhai stated in an interview with the India Today magazine he was 'willing to salaam anyone' in the administration as it was the most important factor which influenced a business from without.

Mukesh knew that his father was going through several pressures and tensions mainly because he had risen as a cult figure among the shareholders, he had once held a meeting of 30,000 shareholders, which was a record in India's corporate history. The gathering was so huge that no hall was big enough, so finally the meeting had to be held in the open ground–Cross Maidan. If he had risen to become a hero in the eyes of his shareholders, the reason was that he had churned out thousands of millionaires out of those who had displayed trust in the initial offers. But being this cult figure also caused a lot of pressures, as he had to prove himself a hero all the time. Mukesh was well aware of these pressures, so he had to devise ways in which he could come true to the expectations of his shareholders without having to undergo such massive pressures; he realized that he could do this by diversifying into newer sectors while expanding the current businesses. He also realized that he had to expand and diversify without having to lose quality; his legendary father had already set an example when way back in 1966, a technical team of the World Bank had admired the textile mill of the Reliance saying that it was 'excellent even by the standards of the developed countries'. Facing these challenges head on, Mukesh was resolved to overcome all these while excelling in terms of performance and achievements. Time has shown that he has no parallels.

In his early career, Mukesh had learnt the value of punctuality, rather being before time, from his father. This passion was evident when the Reliance Refinery at Jamnagar was set up before schedule in 1999, even when several challenges existed, including the earthquake which had flattened the under-construction site there. Not only this, while maintaining world class standards, it cost 30% less than any comparable projects or the international benchmark for any project of this magnitude. Presently, it is the largest of its kind in the world.

Backward Integration

Before delving into this topic, let us understand this term. Any industry needs suppliers and producers which form an important factor in the supply chain for manufacturing of the final product. Other factors involved in the manufacturing may also include other organisations, resources, activities and technologies that play a crucial role in the industrial operations. Sometimes, sourcing supplies from these is either difficult, or time-consuming or costlier. In such a case, a resourceful industry can decide to take over, merge or develop its own supply chain, in part or full. As different industrial operations are under the thumb of the industrialist, it becomes easier for him to get the supplies in time, within the estimated costs and without having to be exploited as fewer middlemen are involved. The savings made in this strategy either add up to the profit or help to make the final product cheaper, which helps to quell competition. Of course, it is not possible for any industry to own up the entire supply chain, but it can be done for a substantial part. Moreover, it may also become feasible to acquire a supplier facility if its production exceeds the consumption in the industry, in which case, provisions will have to be made for its disposal. So, a decision in this regard has to be taken taking all relevant factors into account.

The initiative of backward integration was undertaken by Mukesh during his initial career with the Reliance. First he made forays into polyester fibres, and then into petrochemicals, which were the sources of raw materials for his textiles. In this process, he led the Reliance Industries to create 51 new manufacturing facilities, which were second to none in the world so far as technology was concerned. This backward integration helped Reliance to multiply its capacities in manufacturing.

For Mukesh, only the sky was the limit, as he did not restrict himself to only maintaining what was in his kitty, he took active steps to diversify. One major step in this regard was the establishment of the Reliance Infocomm Ltd. The main focus of this venture was on information and communication technology initiatives. All this while, he was looking for more segments of business into which he could enter, and he sighted his chances in games, especially cricket. Mukesh bought up the team 'Mumbai Indians' to take part in the Indian Premier League (IPL). He has major stakes in the retail business also, as this book will unfold in the pages to follow.

The five main segments that the Reliance presently operates include exploration and production, refining and marketing, petrochemicals, retail, and telecommunications. It is ranked among the top global companies, and is India's most valuable company if considered by market value.

The Tough Challenge

Mukesh and Anil faced a tough time in the business in 1986 following the incident when Dhirubhai suffered a paralytic stroke. They were in their twenties, and the competitors, suppliers, vendors and debtors took them for children; nobody was willing to trust them for their capabilities. It was a challenging time of adversity, and it depended on the budding youths how they made the most out of this opportunity; and they did well enough. The challenge that lay ahead of them was to sustain and also grow at a time when they were devoid of any guidance that they needed.

This was a period of learning for Mukesh, and he made the most of it. He has confirmed that these years were very precious so far as learning the business tactics is concerned; everything was at stake, and they emerged the winner; and they could do this through sticking to the core values that they had learnt in the family.

When Dhirubhai was recovering from his devastating illness, he is said to have described this as the 'era of tempering steel'. He compared the situation with the typical Indian crab story, and described it as an essential part of life. Even in those tough times, Dhirubhai termed the adversaries as the well-wishers of the company.

Mukesh faced difficulty especially from the lenders who, finding Dhirubhai in bed, wanted their money back even before the term it was due. Initially, Reliance tried to convince these lenders, but then they made up the mind to pay back whoever wanted their money back. This brought back the trust the lenders reposed in the company before Dhirubhai's illness. Mukesh and Anil made sure that they never defaulted in payment whatever the situation.

This was also the situation when many people felt that everything was over for Reliance and the young Ambanis would not be able to deal with the massive level of the company's operations. People were so pessimistic about the company that they felt that even if Dhirubhai recovered, he would not be back in working as he was earlier. It was a trying time especially for Mukesh, as he was the elder one; it was a crucial time, because managing to survive through it would simply mean realization of dreams and aspirations a little later. It is said that they were underestimated as 'kids', but they never let that dishearten them; they took it as a God-given opportunity which they must avail.

Mukesh, in particular, was very optimistic that he could tackle this critical situation. Being an engineer, he used to say that Newton's third law had to be kept in mind that every action has an equal and opposite reaction. This was the reason that the more people pushed them down, the more they sprang back. They were determined to prove everybody wrong; and time is a witness that they did it in style.

The values ingrained in Mukesh include the spirit of determination and commitment and ultimate belief in God. He has also inherited the belief in fate, destiny and Karma, without having to forget that the Lord has put the right to act in the human's capacity, and everybody gets the result as the fruit of his action. So, it was essential to work without having to think much of the fruit of the action. Taking an action is an important part of life, and this is the thing that Mukesh believes, and he tries to inculcate this value in all those who are concerned with the Reliance directly or indirectly.

Though there is much about Mukesh in public domain, yet he works as an enigma, in a mysterious, difficult-to-understand way, and he is credited with the spectacular growth of the Reliance Group of Companies ever since he moved into action. He speaks little about himself, and this is the reason that it is difficult to gather much data about his personal life from his end. Yet much about him can be known from the bits of information he gives and from the facts and ideology about the company he runs.

Political Favors

We have in the earlier pages described how Dhirubhai Ambani favored good relations with those in power, and it benefited him to expand exponentially. Mukesh treaded in his father's steps. He has been in good books of the political masters, without fervor or favor; however, he has especially bonded well with the Modi government, and rides the waves in the light of the government's vision of a self-reliant India. Mukesh has aligned his business policies with Modi's vision how India could progress and become an economic power.

This government has been particularly harsh on corruption as well as on the rich, especially those in financial trouble due to their mismanagement of the funds and loans they took for their business from the state-owned financial organisations and government contracts. The harshness of the government was very obvious when in 2016 it passed a bankruptcy law that made it harder for these people to protect their assets from the creditors. These delinquent borrowers were at the receiving end in the courts of law too, which took a severe view of this. There is a long list of billionaires who have suffered owing to this strict policy, and they include Anil Ambani, Vijay Mallya, Nirav Modi, Ruia brothers and others.

Mukesh, on the other hand, presents himself favorable to Modi's vision of a self-reliant, modern, investment-friendly India. Mukesh has been in touch with Modi right from 1990s, when Modi was yet to emerge on the national scene. His stature be can gauged from the fact that he can meet Modi as and when he wishes, rather he is also invited for consultation at the PM's residence. Mukesh does all that is in his right to realize the dream. Modi abolished Article 370 of the Constitution of India making Kashmir an integral part of India promising to people that it could modernize and develop the state greatly; and Mukesh immediately sent a team of professionals looking avenues for investment there. This is the kind of things Mukesh does to participate in the country's development and modernization while remaining in the goods book of the political bosses.

Cultivation of Values

Dhirubhai was very particular about the cultivation of values so far as his children were concerned. High or low, he paid a keen interest on these aspects of life, as he considered values as the very basis of life and without which life could not sail smoothly. Despite being very busy with his business, he never lost sight of how his children were growing.

Self-belief is the main quality of an entrepreneur, feels Mukesh. He once shared his experience that narrates how the Reliance Group went public. For their expansion plan, they needed money, and it was not possible to raise money from traditional sources without having to explain the plans in detail, and there was every chance to be rejected. The banks relied more on the hard data rather than the ambitious planning. It was the spirit of self-belief that made Dhirubhai raise money from the capital market and return it to the investors with a sizeable profit. He had foreseen India as a land of great opportunities, and he wanted to utilize the opportunity that lay ahead.

Dhirubhai believed in having a different kind of company, and Mukesh continues to believe in these ethos. The Reliance Group was able to transform the mindset of people on how they look at business. It was the Reliance Group which propelled the capital market in 1985, and then others followed in their footsteps, bringing about a paradigm change in the business environment of the country.

When asked what makes the Reliance Group a successful company, he cites several reasons. One is that it builds lasting relationships with the employees and all those the company is concerned with. Many of the people keep working for the company over decades; they feel confident that the company will stand by them when they need it most, and the Reliance has displayed this spirit during the testing times of Covid-19. The other factor is much related to the first. That is, the methods, processes and systems that the Reliance Group builds and operates are implemented, not with the owners in mind, but with the people and workers in mind. These ethos, together with the basic values, make all the difference. Its outcome has been glorious. The Reliance Group entered the polyester field when all the big names were already in it, including the Birlas, Modis, Singhanias and several multinationals, except of course the Tatas, but the Reliance Group has been able to leave the biggest impression on this business. Mukesh explains even this success saying that the Reliance likes to invest in businesses of the future and in talent. They are ready to go an extra mile in case they are able to see talent.

Mukesh has taken after his father in this aspect also. While he builds up and expands his father's empire, he does not lose sight of his ideology too. He equally pays attention to the kind of values his children are cultivating. He has personally experienced the adventurous journey that his father made from a mere gas station attendant to a business tycoon, a journey in which they had to live in a chawl, travel in public buses and live like any other ordinary lower-middle class family gradually transforming to higher standards of living, he is anxious enough that his children should cultivate good values, because he believes that values are the basic things in life, without them, success is only an illusion. This was the reason that in the initial years, he made his son to go to school in a general bus so that he could realize the harsh realities of life and how ordinary people live; these people may be ordinary and numerous, but they play a vital role in the success stories of the counted few. It is also said that he made his son travel in the second class at one time, only for this purpose.

Mukesh Ambani exhibits a lavish lifestyle. He can always be seen in decent and elegant clothing and lives in the skyscraper home Antilia, located in South Mumbai, overseeing the Arabian Sea. Antilia was rated as the costliest residential property by the renowned Forbes magazine, and was valued at US $ 1 billion. This 27-storey building is complete with a helipad, a 160-car garage, a private movie theatre, a swimming pool and a fitness center, among all other facilities which a grand house like his is expected to have; and it requires a staff of 600 for maintenance.

Mukesh leads a happily married life. His life partner Nita Ambani steals the limelight whenever she appears in public. The two met for the first time after Dhirubhai saw her in a dance performance in which she took part. This meeting fructified into solemnization of marriage, and now they make one of the most celebrated couples. Mukesh is also known for the most luxurious gifts to his beloved; for an instance, in 2007, he gifted her Airbus A319 on her 44th birthday, it costs US $ 60 million. This airplane is customized with a capacity of 180 passengers, a living room, a bedroom, satellite television, Wi-Fi, sky bar, Jacuzzi and an office among others.

Mukesh and Nita have two sons–Anant and Akash, and a daughter Isha. Isha and Akash are twins.

Mukesh is a big fan of movies; he has said in an interview that he watches three movies a week as 'you need some amount of escapism' in life. He is also known for his philanthropy.

Building Relationships

Mukesh is known for everlasting, perennial relationships. Once he forges a friendship, it is for life. This is the reason that many of his childhood friends are still working with him. He and Anand Jain studied together from class VI, who later went on to study commerce. He now heads the Reliance effort in SEZ. He met Manoj Modi at the UDCT and now heads the retailing venture. Mukesh vividly recalls the names of many of his friends, who may not be working with him, but his bonds with them continue unabatedly.

The same is the case with his workers. He accepts his employees, vendors and shareholders like his friends; he deals with them in such a way that he appears more like a family head; and this is the reason that people like to be dedicated and loyal to him.

Wealth

It is simply beyond imagination how much Mukesh earns; you put any figure today, and it will become redundant tomorrow, so fast is his fortune rising as on date. His wealth mainly comes from the RIL, he is its chairman and managing director; and together with his family, he controls more than 43% of it. In addition, he also receives dividends, a salary and fees as the director. He also holds a stake in the Reliance Industrial Infrastructure and holds some valuable private investments including a gas pipeline.

Learning from Mukesh Ambani

The foundation for Mukesh's success was laid by his father, but what he did to make the Reliance Group the most dazzling company in the world, the credit for this accomplishment should go to him. He himself has revealed the mantra to his success, and it would be interesting to know what he says, and what we can learn from him to taste success in life. His philosophy for success can be gauged from Oprah Winfrey's quote that he shared recently: "If you look at what you have in life, you'll always have more. If you look at what you don't have in life, you'll never have enough." Let us know what Mukesh recommends for success in business:

- The customer is the boss. However high or wealthy you are, the customer remains your boss; and Mukesh advises that a business must never take a step which can cause a loss to his customer. A satisfied customer is your best advertisement, he will bring in more, and a dissatisfied customer will cause multiple problems for you. Therefore, you must always take decisions keeping the interests of the customer in mind.
- Define your goal. For success in business and life, it is essential that the goal is clear to you, and then you must put in all possible labor for achieving it. In his speech at Nasscom, Mukesh said that it is inevitable to set a goal in life to move ahead; in the absence of a clear goal, you may deviate from the path.
- Never fear failures. Failures are part of life, and the greatest of people have faced them. When you are confronted with failures, you must not flee, rather take them head on. To start with, you must start to pinpoint where it arose from and what are its causes. If you are focused to solve the problems being faced by your business, your hard work will never go waste.
- Think positive. The most necessary thing for success in business or job or any aspect of life is positive thinking. If you think positive, you remain positive, this will make your approach positive, and you will be able to taste success rather easily. To achieve this, it is essential that you transmit and spread positivity among people around you.
- Have faith in relation. Business or life are not ex-parte, without relations and partners, you cannot go ahead, as they play a direct or indirect role. For success in

business, it is essential to create fine relations and you must have faith in people. Your faith in relations will transform your life, but this cannot be done blindly, so it is equally essential that you identify the reliable people, because it is their company that will help create the Reliance.

Here is what he said about his learning for success. We quote his words: "My first lesson to the youth is, dream big, align your passion and purpose in life with your goal. If you focus on goal, you will overcome all obstacles. If you focus on obstacles, you will never reach your goal. My second lesson–there is no substitute for hard work, even more important is pursuing excellence and be the best, not just the best in India, but in the whole world. My third lesson— is it is very important to be positive and optimistic in life. Dismiss the prophets of doom. Have self-confidence, believe in yourself, and above all, believe in India, because this country gives every Indian an opportunity to realize his dreams. And I think the best of India is yet to come."

❑

The First Business Family

Nita Ambani

A woman is said to be behind the success of a man. In case of Mukesh, he was already a successful man, and many thought that a wife for him would be more of an ornament, but so was not going to be the case. Mukesh is married to Nita Ambani. Dhirubhai had spotted Nita at a dance performance where she took part. She is a trained Bharatnatyam dancer, and he saw that she would be a perfect match for his elder son. Time has shown that, like scores of Dhirubhai's decisions, this decision too has proved right. She is the daughter of a Birla group executive and grew up in the middle-class atmosphere in suburban Mumbai. She possesses an undergraduate degree in commerce. She had ambitions and aspired not to be a mere housewife, as normally happens to the wives of the well-known businessmen. And Mukesh let loose all bonds for her, and she has proved worthy of her husband's trust.

Married in 1985, Nita joined for a diploma in special education and also worked as a teacher for a few years. We Indians are known for judging others, and they were no different when it came to Nita, especially her working as a teacher; they reasoned that a lady of her status did not need to work as a mere teacher if at all she needed to work. However, Mukesh thought quite differently. He rather encouraged her as she found her work very interesting. Of this tenure, Nita once shared an experience when, as a teacher, she was offered by a student's parent two tickets to the stadium for a match in the 1987 World Cup, which she declined, and the parent sighted her sitting in the VIP stand during the match, only then he realized what she was though working as an ordinary teacher because of her passion for teaching. The Reliance Group was one of the sponsors of the series.

This stint as a teacher did not last long when in 1991, Nita gave birth to premature twins (Isha and Akash), following a difficult IVF pregnancy. She was forced to take a complete break from her work for almost six years. And now was the time for her to swing back into action. Dhirubhai and Mukesh were already confident of her talent, so they entrusted her a job she herself felt not confident about. It was about building a company township at Jamnagar in Gujarat, where the Reliance was building a massive refining complex. "How can I supervise it? I have no experience in this field," she thought nervously, but the Reliance patriarch believed in her.

Once Nita confirmed her participation, she took it head on. She involved herself in the project completely, looking into every fine detail, to the extent that she often supervised where the trees were to be planted and what size of windows would be suitable for the residences. Going into such details required that she be at the project site frequently enough, so she commuted to it two to three times a week. At times, she felt odd as she was the only woman to be present, and all workers often addressed her 'Sir', she recalled.

It was during the course of this project that she saw from close quarters how the Reliance ideology worked. She learnt that the targets in the company were well divided into long-term, short-term and immediate goals and deadlines, and these were sacrosanct. And these goals and deadlines were specified after a prolonged deliberation keeping with the prevailing conditions, and then measures were taken so that the goals could be realized well before the stipulated dates. The probability of any natural calamity too was kept in view. This was the reason that the Reliance Group has seen a number of its projects being completed well before the deadline and at a lower cost. The Jamnagar project was the first for Nita, but it too was completed before time, despite the fact that a devastating cyclone caused much damage to the site. Today, this site is a stupendous splendidly planned township lined with trees, which are home to diverse birds, and is meant for 17,000 residents. And in the vicinity of this township is a mango orchard having close to 1, 00, 000 trees, which has turned the entire township into a dream colony.

Success is like a habit; all those who inculcate this habit know how to get it and how to plan for it. Nita has proved to be one such fellow. Feeling confident from her achievement at Jamnagar, now she wanted to work on her dream K-12 project (an educational institution comprising from the Kindergarten to Class 12), and she needed to build it up from scratch. Today, the Dhirubhai Ambani International School has over 1,000 students and 150 teachers and other staff, and is now ranked among the top schools of Mumbai (her children have studied here).

Nita has often been criticised that she has done precious little for the common and poor masses; to counter this, she conducts evening classes for street kids in this elite school.

It appears that Mukesh involves Nita in projects in which he cannot give time, and she takes it as an opportunity to prove her mettle. Of late, she has come to enjoy these challenges, this proclivity has brought her even more opportunities to prove. So, this is a cycle which with every rotation brings her into limelight, more brilliant than ever before. One case in point is the entry of the Reliance in the sports arena. In 2008, the Reliance bought an IPL (Indian Premier League) team – Mumbai Indians, and acquired such iconic players as Sachin Tendulkar. In the ensuing championships, it was thought that the Mumbai Indians would hoist the flag of its glory, it rather floundered not only on the first occasion, but also on the next. This did not go well with Mukesh, and she looked for someone who could manage the team overcome its problems. And what better name than that of Nita he could choose.

Nita was nervous in the beginning, as sport was a new field for her, and she did not know much about it. And then she worked as she is wont to. She completely immersed herself, studying every fine detail to pinpoint the problem. She made herself a sort of a permanent fixture on the team. She could be sighted with the team quite often. And the result was scintillating: the Mumbai Indians went on to win the next two IPL Championship titles. Sachin Tendulkar has admitted that Nita's presence and involvement in the team made a 'huge difference'. He has also recalled how the team members were given opportunities to bond with each other, which worked wonders with the performance. In one of such occasions, even Mukesh was present, and their presence has an inspiring impact on all factors of the team. For the Reliance, it is not enough to own a team; winning is a prestige game for them. And they can do all that is possible for this purpose. And now the Reliance Group has made forays into different games including basketball, tennis and football, and Nita is the motivating factor behind this. She states that sports and education cannot be isolated from each other, both should go hand in hand. She is not happy with the lack of sports infrastructure in the country, and bemoans that we cannot produce Olympians unless the facilities are created.

Nita also has interest in art and culture, especially in conservation of Indian arts. We have already told you that she is a trained classical dancer in Bharatnatyam. She has also taken up the cudgels to make the Indian arts popular abroad, and she works with the help of the Reliance Foundation in this. This organization sponsored an exhibition of traditional Pichwai paintings of Shrinathji, the Ambani family deity, at the Art Institute of Chicago five years ago. This organization has also funded the events of different artists in foreign locations.

Nita has evinced her basic interest in art when she planned an exhibition space for travelling art shows in a large convention center, that she planned on a massive 19-acre plot adjoining her school in Mumbai. To be completed in 2018, this convention center will include different facilities including a 2,000-seat theatre, retail spaces, offices and residences.

Nita is very active. When she involves herself in any project, she sinks herself in it fully and is ready to breach all boundaries for its sake. The students' parents have seen her standing at the gate of the Ambani School to see who came to take the children back home. This was the kind of dedication she has for her work. Her inclination to such a height of activeness has often motivated Mukesh to assign more responsibilities to her, and she has come out the winner in all of them. She sometimes feels the pressure of her activeness, to tackle which she likes to take to meditation, which only gives her more energy to be active, or rather hyperactive. She has become active especially after the family feud with Anil Ambani was settled into the division of the family fortune.

It is her being active that she has taken over different programmes and functions of the company. When the gala function was held to roll out the much awaited 4G phone service, attended by 37,000 staff on site, and over 75,000 more through a video link, it was all managed by none other than Nita. And the wonder is, this new project doesn't carry the name of Reliance attached to it, it is simply Jio (live life), though its patriarch is well known.

When Nita was asked why it deviated from the practice, she smiled and stated that it was time for the company to enter a 'brave new world' and to 'break away from the old'.

In her working style, Nita is accessible to the staff, rather she likes to mingle with them freely. She is a keen watcher as well as an anxious mother when she mentors her two sons. Her 'soft touch' wins hearts for the Reliance. She may be the non-executive director in the Reliance, yet the buzzword seems to be 'Bhabhi', an affectionate term often used for a friend's wife. If Shobha De, a writer and publisher, describes Nita the 'first lady of Indian business', nothing can be nearer the truth.

Nita has grown to include diverse duties. She has to divide her time looking after different entities, like the Mumbai Indians, Reliance Foundation, Ambani School and others; and with her activeness, she is able to do justice to all these portfolios. She is rather like the 'spotlight' in contrast to her husband being the 'floodlight', in her own words.

Nita founded the Reliance Foundation in 2010, which is a company-funded project. It looks after education and healthcare, but has often been criticized for looking after the interests of the elite classes, so it is dismissed for any philanthropy work for the masses. In response to this criticism, Nita asks these critics to look at her Bharat India Jodo project, which seeks to bridge the rural-urban divide across 12 states of India and works in 531 villages.

Nita is also an ideal mother. She likes to supervise over her children, without interfering in their interests and hobbies. She respects their sentiments and allows them leverage whenever they want to implement any new idea. She supported when Anant wanted to set up an animal shelter at Jamnagar. In fact, the entire Ambani family is a wildlife enthusiast and visits safaris all over the world. Their favorite is Botswana's Moremi Game Reserve.

The Ambani family lives in Antilia, a 27-storey skyscraper, and it was built under Nita's supervision. In an interview which she gave in 2013, Nita says that she likes to cook herself whenever she has free time at her disposal, and Isha is a better cook than her. Speaking about her husband, she says that he is always in the inspiring mode and stands by her when she is busy with any project. She further says that they enjoy a fantastic bonding between them, as if they were partners. They respect each other's views and share the dreams. We have dreams for the family, and as they concern our children, we would like them to tread the path we create for them. When she was asked if she could give a suggestion or two about how Mukesh should conduct his business, she says that she doesn't think she is capable of that, but she admits that they have learnt much from the life's experiences, and she has learnt much from her husband. Speaking about what she likes about her husband, she says that she likes his simplicity and optimism.

Nita also reveals that she was brought up among 11 sisters, Mamta of them being her own sister, and others being cousins. Nita says that she was brought up in a joint family and we all believed in the power of education and paid due attention to women's equality and empowerment. She says that she sinks in the old reminiscences whenever she visits her paternal home at

Santacruz. She feels proud of her past days and of the foundation that was laid in those days which continue to inspire her even today.

Akash Ambani

Akash, born in October 1991, studied economics at Brown University, and is married to Shloka Mehta. She has studied anthropology at Princeton University, New Jersey, and then received her Masters in Law and Anthropology at the London School of Economics (LSE). Their marriage in March 2019 was a sizzling, opulent three-day wedding programme.

Akash is already on board of his father's company, and is being groomed to take over the reins of the Reliance in the days to come. He is being given more responsibility as he grows, and he has already worked for the telecom arm of the Reliance in Mumbai. His current title is Chief of Strategy. Like his father, he also takes interest in games, and has been sighted at sports events including the face-off between India and Pakistan in the ICC Cricket World Cup. He has also displayed his skills in the popular soccer video game Fifa 2019 when he demonstrated the Jio set-top box for its capability. Akash is also fond of cars, and his collection includes Bentley Bentayga, India's most expensive SUV, Benz G-Wagen and Range Rover among others.

Akash is a great fan of his father, Mukesh. He terms him his 'hero' and praises him for his unwavering work ethics in his sixties. What he admires his father most is his welcome to new ideas and treats everybody with respect, despite him being in an enviable position of being the richest business tycoon. Akash hopes to follow in his father's glorious footsteps.

Anant Ambani

Anant, born on 10 April, 1995 and a graduate of Brown University, in Providance, Rhode Island, suffered from chronic asthma, so he was put on a medication of steroids. However, this medication is known to cause increased hunger which, in case of Anant, led to weight gain. He has displayed determination to lose excess weight, and he achieved this through diet and exercise, especially long walks. He is said to have walked almost 18 km regularly. He lost 108 kg in less than 18 months. There are many people looking to lose weight, and this could be an inspiration for them.

Anant is also known for his love for pets. He has an exotic pet collection, and he has posed with his pet Alaskan Malamute. As it belonged to a very cold climate of Alaska, Anant has ensured that a section of his room has a controlled climate so that his pet feels comfortable in the hot and humid climate of the coastal Mumbai. He is also fond of luxury cars, and he has been spotted driving them himself. His proud car collection includes Rolls-Royce Cullinan, Rolls-Royce Phantom Drophead Coupe, BMWi8 among others. Anant is close to his mother Nita and often works in her charitable organisation – Reliance Foundation, to help those in need. He was recently in news for his donation of over US $ 260,000 to workers affected by the Covid-19 pandemic. He is also religious and has visited several temples including the Siddhivinayak Temple, Mumbai, Lord Balaji Temple at Tirupati, Kedarnath Temple and Badrinath Temple. He is on the temple committee of the Badrinath-Kedarnath temples, and has also donated a white elephant for the god's ride at Tirupati. Like his elder brother, Anant is also fond of cricket, and can be spotted in big matches. He is a fan of the Mumbai Indians, an IPL team owned by his father.

Isha

Isha was born on 23 October, 1991 and has taken higher education at Stanford Graduate School of Business (2018) and is presently happily married to Anand Piramal. She also takes active part in the Reliance business.

Kokilaben Ambani

Kokilaben lives with Mukesh. She was married to Dhirubhai Ambani in 1955. When he left for Aden, he made arrangements to get her there. When she was on the way, Dhirubhai telephoned and informed that he had bought a car for her and he was coming to fetch her. Just guess what colour is the car, he said in the conversation. Kokilaben was trying to guess, when Dhirubhai revealed: "Don't guess, it's black like me." she reminisces about their long association. Whenever he started a new project, he would seek her advice, though she was not able to say much, mainly because of her limited knowledge of English. To overcome this limitation, he hired an English tutor for her. Not only this, he would get her to inaugurate anything new.

Kokilaben has revealed in an interview that whenever Dhirubhai had plans to visit another city, he would assign her the job of gathering information about it. He also recalls that when they bought a new aircraft, he asked her to invite her friends for a flight.

She has sailed in rough waters on two occasions in her life, the first was when she lost her dear husband due to a massive heart attack, and the second was when she had to divide the Reliance between the two sons. As memory to her husband and their long association, a hospital has been built in Mumbai in 2009, named Dhirubhai-Kokilaben Ambani Hospital.

Kokilaben acted wisely dividing the assets between Mukesh and Anil, which otherwise could have become a massive controversy, but she secured an amicable agreement between the two brothers through her motherly command. Not only this, when Anil was facing a tough time, she forced Mukesh to help his brother. It will be interesting to see what role she plays because Anil has come to find himself in troubles after troubles.

Vimal Ambani

When I like to include this name in this part of the book, you may be surprised. Vimal Ambani is Mukesh's cousin, the son of his elder uncle Ramnikbhai. In fact, Dhirubhai entered the business by naming his textile brand as Vimal (later Only Vimal), after his name. Presently, Vimal is the head of the Tower Overseas Ltd. He started this company about 24 years ago, and it deals in real estate investment, stock brokerage and startup investment. In addition to this, he is also a non-executive director of the Syntex Industries Ltd. He also functions as a director of several other companies. Prior to it, he looked after the textile division of the Reliance Industries in the capacity of the Chief Executive.

It would be worthwhile to tell about Ramnikbhai Ambani. Until 2014, he was part of the Reliance Industries Board, and he remained part of it until the age of 90, when he was replaced with Nita Ambani.

And the House

The Ambani family lives in the Antilia overlooking the Arabian Sea. The Antilia, the world's costliest house, is a 27-storey mansion built over 4, 00,000 sq feet. The first six floors are used as the parking space in which as many as 168 big cars can be parked conveniently. There is a 50-seater auditorium to watch movies. Mukesh Ambani lives in the topmost but one floor. There are 600 employees, including 40 body-guards, to look after the house, and these employees are paid well. The Antilia has a manager at each floor to look after the facilities there.

Who will be the lucky one to inherit the wealth? Well, as of date, it is yet unclear. Isha and Akash have already been inducted into the company and are holding key executive roles in the telecom business. Anant too is being inducted gradually as he matures.

Key Takeaways

- Mukesh Ambani was born in the British colony, Colony of Aden, now Yemen. His father, Dhirubhai Ambani, decided to leave Yemen as it was now independent and risky for any outsider.
- Mukesh recalls how his childhood was spent in fun and learning. Mukesh Ambani studied chemical engineering at the Institute for Chemical Technology (then named as UDCT), Matunga and graduated in Chemical Engineering in 1979.

- Ambani's father never looked for marks and school but always asked him to gain as much practical knowledge as he could, through annual field trips to the village and from the family business.
- In order to learn the practical skills necessary to manage bossiness, Dhirubhai Ambani wanted Mukesh to return from Stanford University.
- Even though Mukesh wished to remain and finish his degree, he requested if they might start the plant 18 months later. However, Dhirubhai refused, and Mukesh had to return to India as a result of this.
- From Yemen to India, Dhirubhai Ambani relocated in 1958, just a year after Mukesh Ambani was born.
- Without any revenue or clients, he founded Reliance Commercial Corporation.
- Dhirubhai Ambani and Kokilaben Ambani had four children, the oldest son is Mukesh Ambani, followed by Anil Ambani, Nina Ambani, and Dipti Ambani.
- Reliance Industries was founded by Dhirubhai and Mukesh Ambani.
- Mukesh Ambani was expected to start working at age 17 and assist his father in splitting the workload of the family business as the eldest son.
- He requested in-person meetings and close-knit conversations within the venture group.
- In a year and a half, the Patalganga project was finished, resulting in the creation of PFY in 1982.
- Additionally, he was appreciative of his father's view of him as a first-generation partner rather than a second-generation inheritor.

- On a bustling Mumbai Street, Mukesh Ambani proposed to Nita Ambani. In 1985, the pair married after becoming acquainted through Mukesh's father.
- Dhirubhai Ambani had his first stroke in 1986 and died in 2002 as a result of his second stroke.
- In an interview with Simi Garewal, Mukesh Ambani, the businessman Dhirubhai's son, recalled the horrific event and explains how Mukesh was being reassured by Dhirubhai Ambani that he was fine and would survive.
- Reliance Industries' founder and chairman, Dhirubhai Ambani, died in 2002.
- While his younger son Anil Ambani served as vice-chairman, his older son Mukesh Ambani rose to the positions of chairman and managing director.
- Between the Ambani brothers, there was a rift brought on by a lack of will that resulted in a huge argument later and distribution of assets by Kokilaben Ambani.

❑

Reliance Foundation

The companies engage themselves in a large variety of businesses and services with the primary motive of earning profits, and these profits are earned from the society directly or indirectly. In this sense, it is generally viewed that these companies should also carry out some social responsibility which will benefit the society. This is called corporate social responsibility or CSR. It is in the interests of different players, including the government, society, citizens, and the companies themselves. When CSR benefits customers to raise the income levels, it ultimately benefits the companies as their customer widens. It has also been found in a survey that the customers favor those companies which are involved in CSR. Despite such a simple concept, there is no universally agreed definition for CSR. A common approach, on part of the companies, is giving monetary donations and aid to non-government organisations (NGOs) working in areas such as education, housing, health, culture, social welfare, environment and cleanliness, among others, but it does not include political contributions and event sponsorships. The CSR rules, which came into effect on 1 April, 2014, state that companies with a net worth of Rs. 500 crore or revenue of Rs. 1,000 crore or net profit of Rs. 5 crore or more should spend 2% of their average profit in the last three years on social development-related activities such as sanitisation, education, healthcare and poverty alleviation, among others, which are listed in the Schedule VII of the Rules.

On its part, the Reliance has also entered CSR to contribute to the society in diverse fields such as education, rural transformation, health, sports for development, disaster response, arts, culture and heritage, and urban renewal, which it tries to do through the Reliance Foundation, set up in 2010, and headed by Nita Ambani. The vision document of the Reliance Foundation reads: "At Reliance Foundation, our vision is to build an inclusive India by pioneering a holistic model to address our nation's multifaceted development challenges, and contribute to its collective aspirations. Central to our philosophy is the commitment to enhance the quality of life of people from marginalised and vulnerable communities, by empowering them and catalysing change through innovative and sustainable solutions. Our steadfast endeavour is to create replicable and scalable models of development through an integrated approach in the true Reliance spirit of maximising societal value for all, and making it a movement."

It makes a bid for India's inclusive development, with a comprehensive development approach. Its objective is to create and support meaningful activities through innovative institutions to address some of India's most pressing developmental challenges. It lays significant stress on leveraging technology for developmental solutions and tries to reach the affected communities through trained professionals. Over the years, its initiatives have evolved keeping in with the dynamic needs of the communities. It has also established partnerships with organizations that have the technical expertise and experience to undertake various programmes in the identified focus areas of operation. Its important activities are in five sectors, as enumerated below:

- Rural transformation. The Bharat-India Jodo is a programme aimed at marginal farmers, including information service programmes under which technical assistance is brought to farming and fishing villages.
- Education. The Reliance Foundation grants scholarships under the Dhirubhai Ambani Scholarship Programme, which was started in 1996 with a focus on Maharashtra and Gujarat, and has now spanned its wings nationwide. It grants scholarships for various levels like Jio Scholarship for graduates and Dhirubhai Ambani Scholarship at various school levels. It also supports 13 schools, including the Dhirubhai Ambani

International School and establishes universities in partnership with the London School of Economics (LSE). It also proposes to set up a Jio Institute at Karjat.

- Health. The Foundation sponsors the Drishti programme which provides newspapers in Braille for the blind. It also runs the country's largest corona transplant programme and has developed the Sir HN Reliance Foundation Hospital and Research Centre in Mumbai.
- Arts, culture and heritage. The Foundation sponsors events celebrating and continuing the cultural heritage of India, such as Ustad Zakir Hussain's annual concert in memory of his father, Abbaji and the Elephanta Festival on Elephanta Island of Mumbai. It has also held the nationwide arts and essay competitions which also involved visually impaired participants.

In addition to these, the Reliance Foundation works in cooperation with other philanthropies and NGOs on collaborative initiative; for example, in 2012, it partnered with the television show Satyamev Jayate to provide a grant to Muktangan Rehabilitation Centre in Mumbai to help street children.

For its activities, the Reliance Foundation has also won several awards including the Rashtriya Khel Protsahan Puraskar in 2017, Billionth Asia Award 2017, CSR Community Initiative Award 2017, CSR Excellence Award, Late VD Joshi Award for Best Ferrocement Structure 2016, CSR Award 2016 for Water Conservation, Agricultural Development and Best Documentary Film,

Porter Prize 2015, and Golden Peacock Award among others.

The Reliance Foundation is included amongst the top spenders on CSR and has held this position for the last several years. The RIL has spent almost 76% of its CSR on education, sanitation and skill development, and has also gone up to spend a sizeable sum on sports development in the country, and this has been cited as Nita Ambani's initiative. The Foundation believes in the power of sports to create positive social impact and is committed to creating a large-scale ecosystem for sports and to train the youth of India to take it up as a vocation.

Despite the efforts being made by the Reliance Foundation, fingers have been pointed against it that it is not doing enough for CSR keeping in with the financial status it enjoys in the country and world.

❑

The Reliance Industries: The Growth Story

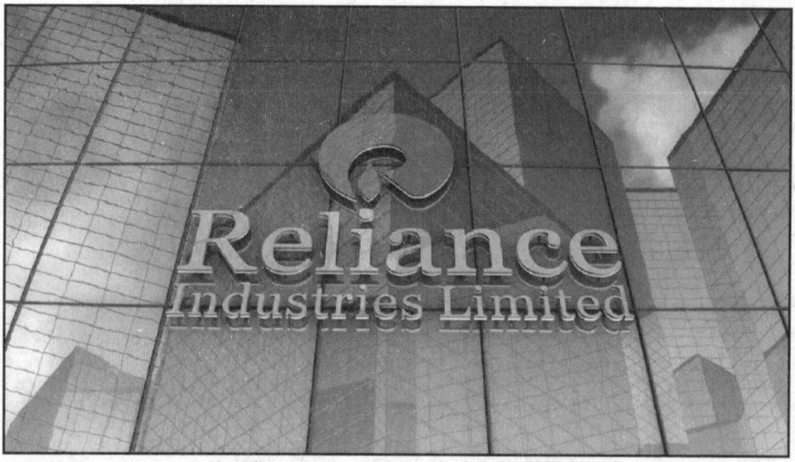

Growth and expansion of the Reliance has been spectacular and amazing. The Reliance Industries Ltd (RIL) is India's largest private-sector company generating a revenue which forms a sizeable percentage of the country's GDP. Its expansion story started with Dhirubhai Ambani at the zenith when in the mid-1960s, he became determined to enter the manufacturing sector coming into competition with his own customers. He went on to set up his first factory in 1966, which proved a success. This success was the outcome of the basic values that he chalked out; one among them was to use technology. He made sure to use the most modern, highly efficient equipment, and this helped him outpace competitors, who often relied on equipment not as modern as his. At this time, the textile scene in the country was dominated by a few business families, and it became difficult for Dhirubhai to market his products, so he decided to set up his own brand Vimal and then Only Vimal through dedicated outlets. This enabled him to sell not only fabrics but also the range of his clothing range, to the extent that he made 'Only Vimal' a viable name in the fashion market.

Entering the Share Market

While Dhirubhai needed to look for more finance to accomplish his expansion plans, the traditional sources of money were eclipsed by the 'old boy' syndrome, and this was hard for him to digest, so he decided to enter the public offering in 1977, and from this point of time, things were going to change for all times to come. The decision to raise money from the stock market was a revolutionary step. He launched the Reliance Textile Industries' initial public offering (IPO) consisting of 2.8 million shares and raised $ 1.8 million. It came to be considered one of the largest in India at that time. This step is called revolutionary because it led to the country's emergence as the regional industrial centre. Here comes in focus the basic value of courage, because he had resolved to circumvent the traditional route of the state for capital investment. Ever since there is no looking back.

This was also the stage when Mukesh and Anil had joined the Reliance Group and had started to contribute in the growth story being scripted at the Reliance Group by their father. These young men had to take up the cudgels in their hands in the aftermath of their father suffering a paralytic attack, though he remained the chairman until his death in 2002. In these years, the company achieved several milestones, including a unit for production of linear alkyl benzene, followed by the opening of a paraxylene plant in 1988, and also started developing a new petrochemicals plant at Hazira, which began production of vinyl chloride monomer and polyvinyl chloride. This was the way in which the company built up its leadership in the market in polyesters and polymers. By 1992, the company had started its full-scale production of high-density polythelene at the Hazira complex as well.

Emergence of the Indian Petroleum Giant

The petroleum sector was nationalized in 1976 following the global oil crisis and with this, this sector was under the strict control of the state-owned companies. These companies did well, however, in the 1990s, the country's oilfields were showing signs of depletion and the country had to become overly dependent on import; all this while, the demand for petroleum was rising exponentially. The state-owned companies were finding it difficult to explore new oilfields.

It was in this state of affairs that in 1991 the Reliance Group decided for vertical integration and set up a new subsidiary: Reliance Refineries Pvt. Ltd. with an intent to enter the petroleum field. This company later changed its name to Reliance Refineries Ltd. and in 1993, launched a public offer, which was going to become India's largest IPO at that time. Along with exploration, the company put in its plans to start developing petroleum products and their marketing, which was to be done through a network of about 1,000 service stations.

To raise capital, the Reliance Group continued to pioneer financing channels in India, and also became the first Indian company to raise capital in the foreign market, in which it issued a Global Depository Receipt (GDR) issue in Luxembourg. The company did not rest at this, and brought another successful GDR issue the following year in 1994. The company used the new capital in part to expand its petrochemicals wing, building the world's largest multi-feed cracker at the Hazira site. The company also added production plants for monoethylene glycol, polyethylene, and purified terephthalic acid. The new units launched production in 1998.

Reliance's opportunity for entry into petroleum refining came in 1997, when the Indian oil industry reached a state of near collapse. Unable to fund further exploration operations, and lacking the capital to expand its existing production, the government was forced to liberalize the sector. In that year, the Reliance Group announced a plan to build one of the world's largest and most modern petroleum refining complexes in Jamnagar, Gujarat, at a cost of some $6 billion. The government agreed to the plan, and granted the company the right to import petroleum directly, rather than going through Indian Oil, which helped the Reliance greatly drive down operating costs.

Constructed in a record time, the Jamnagar site was commissioned in 1999. The site's production capacity was double that of any other Indian refinery and ranked among the top five in the world. The addition of the new facility also placed Reliance at the top rank of the country's private-sector companies. In 2002, Reliance Petroleum was merged into Reliance Industries, which then became one of the country's top three companies, including state-owned entities.

The RIL has also successfully completed its backward integration strategy that has transformed it into India's largest private-sector petrochemicals company, and is behind only the state-owned Indian Oil. Its petrochemicals division is fully integrated and includes exploration and production; refining (the company has built one of the world's largest and most modern refinery complexes at Jamnagar in Gujarat); marketing through a chain of more than 1,000 service stations; and production of petrochemicals including polymers, polyester, polyester intermediaries and others. These chemicals are used to support its continuing textile operations which focus primarily on polyester fabrics. Following the acquisition of the Trevira in 2004, the company has become the world's leading polyester manufacturer, with production levels topping 25 million metres per year. The company's textile range also includes other fabrics such as acrylics and finished garments, which are primarily sold through its dedicated outlets across the country.

It is often alleged that the company prospered and thrived during the license raj in early stages of 1970s and 1980s, especially through manipulation. It is well known that Dhirubhai had built up strong connections in the government, and it appeared to be a key policy of the company, and this inclination was in tune with the policy followed by other business houses.

However, it should be realized that the license raj prevailed for everybody, and not for the Reliance alone. Moreover, getting a license to manufacture does not ensure that everything will fall in place automatically; rather the more important tasks of laying the infrastructure, managing the finances, winning trust of the shareholders, marketing the products remain massive challenges. The business is not limited to obtaining the license alone; and in the present competitive world, you have to be on your toes all the time, follow all the right policies, ensure quality of your product and conduct, only then can you imagine of getting the popular support.

Moreover, the Reliance Group has grown far higher in the period following the license raj than it did during this. Once Anil Ambani remarked, "I don't see any harm in building relationships with people, whether it's my customer or my vendor, whether it's my shareholder or somebody in a position of authority whom we need to convince about our case."

The Reliance Group has built up its edifice on trust; it has won the trust and confidence of all those who are concerned with it, whether they are customers or vendors, investors or debtors. The Reliance Group proudly boosts that no one can blame the company for not having paid what was due. "Nobody can say that we have run away with anybody's money," said Anil Ambani once with a bright shine in his eyes.

The company has grown on the core values that were ingrained by the patriarch – Dhirubhai Ambani. And these core values are very simple to follow, only you need to be consistent in following them; they are: be humble, be down to earth, be simple and be approachable.

Getting a license during the license raj could only be a meaningful exercise only when a sustainable business could be established. This can be done when different competencies can be built by harnessing the resources, direct or indirect. These competencies include how to nurture talent, how to gather a team to achieve the goal and how to raise money to get going. When Mukesh was launched into the business, he found that the business houses operated as per the whims of the so-called experts; all this was like a close system. Mukesh studied this system thoroughly, and from this, he developed his own ideas, as Dhirubhai had given him a free hand to set up the industry in chemicals. His ideas came to a conclusion that he needed to build more confidence with people at different levels, and taking cues from what he had learnt from his father, he determined to invest in the future and in the talent, and not in the stale business practices that were going on in the industry at that time. He preferred to have an open system. He decided to take all those concerned in confidence rather than keeping everything secret among a few top people. So, he went for the SOPs and SOCs (standard operating procedures and standard operating conditions). This ensured that all those concerned with execution were in know of the in-things, and this would also give them a sense of belongingness and ownership, which was an essential factor to groom a team.

It had been a Reliance practice from the very beginning to invest in the talent, and this paid off well whenever they decided to expand to other sectors, as diverse as the group is as of today. Also, the basic tenet of the company from the initial stages was to become internationally competitive. They relied on experts but to a limited extent, and put more emphasis on building their own core teams. For example, in 1980s, they hired experts from the

American company Du Pont and put some 25-year-old managers under them to see how they worked, planned and executed things in the chemical processes. This set up ensured that the person at the top had ideas which had to be implemented keeping in tune with the best practices being followed in the world.

A great advantage of this open system was that the talent can be retained, as personnel feel that they have something to do which they thought about, and that they had freedom to take decisions. Making people to take decisions also made them responsible, their amenability rose from this factor, and this went on to benefit the company overall.

Mukesh views the era of 1980s-90s as the one in which the Indian businesses focused their competencies on basic things, like building infrastructure, getting supplies and getting sales. These were essential parts, but the Reliance Group also paid attention to one more crucial aspect, that was to build competencies in diverse fields. These competencies helped the company sail through any tough times that it faced and these companies stood in good stead when the company decided to diversify in other fields. Mukesh admits that expansion into other fields did not cause much worry to them as they already had competencies to confront any untoward and unexpected situations that might arise during the course of any new venture. He admits that this competency was crucial, and it is this factor that was underestimated by the competitors.

The Reliance found itself in rough waters in 1985. The top management of the company was being run by three people: Dhirubhai, Rasikbhai and Mukesh. In

1985, Rasikbhai breathed his last and in the following February, Dhirubhai suffered a paralytic stroke. Now, all the pressure was on Mukesh who was supposed to face all the pressures alone. Anil was there to assist him, but he was still new in the field.

These two incidents occurred when the company was in the good books of the investors and lenders, and this situation disturbed everything. As we have narrated before, people started to demand their money even when it was not yet due. It was a situation of do or die. Mukesh realized that until then the company had thrived on the confidence that his father had built up even in the face of adversaries, and he would have to adopt the same approach. He made sure that he paid up whatever was due to anybody, without defaulting even to a single score. And the dividends came. Those who predicted a dooms day for the Reliance returned to the company with more offers, and in a period of about 5 months, Dhirubhai too was reasonably well, and with this, the situation started to sail back to the normal.

Recalling this period, Mukesh states that there was no panic in his mind as they had already created an open system; had it been a secret system, it would have been difficult to proceed ahead because these two mishaps could have deprived the Reliance much wisdom and virtue on which the company depended. In the open system, people on different posts knew what to do in a specific situation, and that made things easy for Mukesh as well as the Reliance. In times of such a calamity, what was required for him to put his head down and execute. And we know that he did it too well. It is especially important because the prevalent thinking in the country was that the Reliance relied more on 'managing the system' rather than having talent of its own, but the Reliance proved it wrong effectively.

Another big challenge for the Reliance came about when the government announced opening up of the economy in the early 1990s. A lot of companies in India found that it would be difficult for them to compete with the best in the international market; but that was not the case with the Reliance. Right since the earliest times, the Reliance Group had put stress on raising its standards to the international level and following standardised practices and processes. They had been doing this even earlier than 1980s when the tariffs were very high at 300%. Even at that time, they built competencies and obsessed themselves with a notion to compete with and beat the Koreans and the Taiwanese who dominated the polyester business.

Any company can expect to compete with and beat the competitors with only better competencies; and it included the scale of the production. Mukesh reminisces that even during the license raj, they had built up a polyester capacity of 75,000 tonnes, while facing all the limitations put up by the licenses. Looking to compete with the world even when put at a disadvantaged position led to building such capacities which the other native competitors could not hope to go for.

When the economy was opened up, it brought great opportunities. The tariffs were brought down to 150% and then to 30% in 1995 and later to 10%, and this was bound to boost the Reliance Group a great deal. They already possessed the infrastructure to compete at the international level, and now all the strings had been loosened. Reducing the tariffs actually benefited the Reliance Group; or we can put it as Mukesh feels about it: "We wanted to be internationally competitive when the tariffs were 300%, but being based in India became a competitive advantage when the tariff fell below 30%."

Existing competencies paid dividends as they had competent people to execute projects. Mukesh says that they have not faced any difficulty in starting any plant or project because of this talent that they had nurtured over time. He feels proud to say that even the biggest companies in the world lack this capacity which they had built up while expanding themselves. This is where an eye on the future and on the talent pays off handsomely.

Much depends on the mindset. There were a number of Indian companies that were doing well, but following their model could not put the Reliance into international competition; so it was decided to look to the international companies and what models and practices they followed in the course. The Reliance Group sourced data, standards and other required information from the international companies, especially those of the US, that being an open society and sourcing data was not much of a problem. Even though the internet age had not yet dawned, but sourcing the data did not pose much problem, as Mukesh sees it. Of course, this data did not come for free, sometimes it needed a large investment, but it was worth the investment, because it helped the Reliance to put the thought process in the right direction.

The mindset makes all the difference. For example, the Reliance Group sourced several managers from public sector enterprises, which are known for their slack manners and execution, but the same manager excelled in execution when they joined the Reliance. Mukesh has termed KK Malhotra as his Guru, who came from a public sector company in 1985.

The vision of the Reliance has been very clear from the very outset how it wishes to nurture talent. The top management of the Reliance Group has believed in the tenet that even ordinary people can do wonders and achieve extraordinary results if they are given a sensible framework. Mukesh feels proud to say that they have been able to do that in industry after industry, and the talent nurtured by them has proved them right.

There are books which narrate all sorts of best practices, and there are research papers which are written from time to time, and all these can guide a person in the best practices and processes which can be adopted to be successful. However, the main thing is to put them into practice. Normally, there is a gap between what is written and what is executed; if this gap is bridged, success is sure to come; and this was precisely the thing that happened with the Reliance. The best practices and procedures were studied keenly and then they were matched with the vision; and then things were studied about what should happen at the shop-floor and what should happen in the market; and in conjunction with all these factors, the strategy should be devised. Ultimate success is achieved when different sorts of practices, methods and processes are synchronised in line with the vision, and the final path to be treaded is set before any action is taken, and there should also be a provision to correct in case things go wrong, and the things destined to go wrong will ultimately go wrong;

however, if you have made provision for them in advance, such things will not prove a stumbling block in the process of marching ahead. The Reliance Group was able to do just this, and the outcome is for all to see.

Diversification

Until the year 2000, the Reliance had no plans to diversify into any other sector other than what concerned their basic textile business; this diversification or backward integration led to include diverse fields, including polyester, plastics, refinery and upstream business of oil and gas. In the late 90s, the Reliance Group was in a good position in these fields; and with huge cash flows, there was much scope to do more. This scope could be in two directions: to further expand the existing business as their current businesses were going to stay for a long time to come, that is, they too were the businesses of the future, and as per the company policy, they wanted to invest in the future businesses. This direction could make their current businesses bigger and global. And the other direction was to encompass more sectors, and it was this direction that was decided upon, and this was how the Infocomm was born.

The foray into the Infocomm was a bit surprising for the watchers because the Reliance Group had missed the bus in early 1990s when the IT (information technology) was supposed to be the future business; more so because at that time, Mukesh was in the Silicon Valley and had noticed what was happening there from close quarters. However, at that time, the Reliance Group was busy in building diverse competencies in the existing business, and it was decided that it was not the optimal time for it to enter a new field. It could have meant deviating its attention from the thing it was still in the process of building, and also could have resulted in biting more than the mouth could take in. Moreover, the IT sector could have demanded to build it from the scratch, needing huge effort, and the top management was not inclined to do that at that time. As Mukesh described this situation as '...we have too much soap on our body and we need to take a bath in the chemicals business'. Initially, Mukesh was in two minds so far venturing into the IT was concerned, and gone to the extent of signing a JV (joint venture) with the Microsoft, but then let it pass up. They decided to keep focus on the business they were already in.

The Reliance Group did not take long to make a big move. By the late 90s, it was a big name in textiles and plastics, and it was at this time that they were looking to diversify, and they were necessitated to do that quickly when the Dow Chemicals announced that it was going to make plastics from E Coli. That could prove to be a great jolt, and an urgent step was required to be taken, as it could have affected their business adversely. In response to this new situation, the Reliance Group entered the biotech business. And as part of it, they went on to include plant biotech, as Dhirubhai saw big opportunities in agriculture, and called it the business of the future.

As part of diversification, the Reliance Group also entered communication, started bidding for cellular licenses; but it was thought that the real value lay not in communication alone, but in the convergence of communication and information, and this is the reason that they prefer to call it Infocomm. This was entirely a new domain for the company, so they looked for talent in this field, and also groomed their own talent to take up the challenge, and we can see the outcome as of date.

Reliance in Telecommunication

When Mukesh and Anil divvied up the Reliance, the Reliance Infocomm fell in the share of the latter. Mukesh saw telecommunication as the business of the future, and wanted to enter this field as soon as could be possible, but in the pact between two brothers, there was a 'non-compete' clause, by which any of them could not enter a business which could be in direct competition to the other. By 2010, Anil was struggling to make his power plants viable for which he needed gas from his elder brother, and it is learnt that it was insisted for the 'non-compete' clause in the agreement be annulled.

In about 2016, only about half of India's population possessed a mobile phone, which simply meant that there was a huge potential to grow in this field, and Mukesh wanted to exploit this, and wanted to this in a style that would shake the existing players in it. The Reliance Group launched Jio, shaking the competitors out of their slumber. The rates were so cheap that it became utterly difficult for the smaller players to continue to retain their customer base. At the launch ceremony, Mukesh stated: "Mobile internet will be the single most defining technology of this century for human development...we feel fortunate to be the ones to bring mobile broadband revolution to 1.2 billion Indians."

Interestingly, Jio's initial wireless spectrum had originally been purchased not by Reliance, but by a smaller player called the Infotel Broadband Service Ltd, which had been acquired by the Reliance a few hours later. Less than 3 years later, the national telecommunication regulator effected a change in the rules to include voice calls as well as data in the spectrum, which greatly benefited the Reliance Group. Had the situation been so at the time of auction, it could have cost almost $ 533 million higher, while the initial auditors' earlier draft of this revealed the difference at as much as $ 3.6 billion. From this can be gauged the extent of the benefit. All along, the Reliance Group maintained that all relevant rules had been abided by so far as the Jio's spectrum was concerned.

As was evident from the very beginning, the Reliance Group hoped to dominate the telecom market, where there were about a dozen of operators. Its main focus was on converting the masses into customers by even suffering some losses, but the increased customer base was bound to bring in rich dividends in the times to come, and with cash reserves flowing with it, this risk could well be taken. Its service in the beginning was as good as free. Time has shown that the estimate was not wrong either.

The Reliance Group took the market with a storm, which was hard to digest for the competitors and their very existence was at stake. Jio's service was practically free, coupled with the offer of a virtually free mobile phone, and the charges being as low as Rs. 7.5 a gigabyte; and the freebies did not stop at this, the voice calls were fully free. This led to a price war. The competitors accused Jio of a predatory behaviour, which was rejected. Of course, this diversification hit hard Anil Ambani among the others. Many fingers pointed that Mukesh took a revenge on his brother, while others supported his move that he was creating a space for his nascent company, comforted by the success that he had earned until then. This step hit Anil so hard that he had to file for bankruptcy in 2019.

This time again, Mukesh came to the rescue of his brother, but not without a collateral, this time, a pair of 99-year leases on office buildings in Mumbai, forcing Anil to shift his office to smaller spaces. The statement published to this effect is said to have been drafted by Mukesh's side without it having been shown to Anil, though it contained several quotations from Anil.

Looking into Agriculture

Dhirubhai had seen great opportunities in agriculture; he had started his business with textile, which is an agricultural product. He had a vision to expand his wings in this field. The problems agriculture faced in India were unique to it, and were different from those prevailing in other countries like the US which had transformed agriculture into a massive earning potential. On the other hand, in India, the economy did not get a chance to develop it into a sustainable value chain which could bring opportunities for the farmers and all those concerned in this sector. Agriculture contributes to about 28% of our GDP (gross domestic product) while it employs 60% of manpower; this simply meant that each agricultural worker's potential was not being utilized optimally. This could be done when our agricultural products would be allowed to raise their standards to the international standards. Raising our agricultural products to the international standards simply meant that a professional approach was needed, especially in marketing the products. The agricultural producers are needed to be given access to market where they can sell their produce, and for this purpose, they will have to raise the standard of their produce. As a matter of fact, many of our agricultural products are not worth the international market where high standards are observed, which our native farmers fail to follow, especially because of their inclination to use chemical fertilizers, pesticides etc.

A major problem of Indian agriculture comprises fragmented landholdings. Generation after generation, the landholdings grow smaller in size, many of which have been rendered unproductive. The Reliance concluded in its findings that the fragmented landholdings can be brought together as one unit through technology.

The Reliance Group studied all relevant aspects of agriculture and made certain conclusions, such as that India's purchasing power rests on food; food remains the primary expenditure, education comes second. The food market in the world is very big, far bigger than the software market. And most importantly, this puts money in the hands of the common farmer who lives in the remote village; but this does wonders to his purchasing power. Imagine a farmer in a remote village enjoying the television and refrigerator in the comfort of his pucca house. When a common farmer has money, the markets zoom; we have seen how sales pick up during and soon after the harvest time; and if there could be devised a way in which a farmer is able to get a regular income round the year, it will boost up all other sectors in the country. In the end, it will play a big role in making India an economic power to contend with, because there will be created a plenty of jobs in the process.

The greatest problem in agriculture that the Reliance felt was the distribution of produce, and if the opportunities in distribution logistics are explored, this sector could give rich dividends. To create this distribution logistics required close to Rs. 25,000 crore, but it found that raising this money was not going to be a problem if investors sensed that an effective distribution network could be established, because the Hindustan Lever had almost failed when it entered agricultural retailing, and this fact could not be lost sight of. The Reliance Group studied where this business house failed, and concluded that contract farming was not the right way to go. So, it developed its own ideology and named it 'contact farming', 'r' was missing from the term, and it carried quite a different connotation.

To deliver the Indian agricultural products with a global standard at a competitive price in the world market required several processes to be put in place. The farms in India are small while those in the US are very expansive where the cost factors are favorable to the produce; but in case of India, the prices of products are low. At the same time, the global demand is for the standardized products, and not for anything, and for this purpose, the global buyer is ready to pay handsomely. The Reliance Group, in its study of a common agricultural product like potato, found that a farmer in North India sells it for Rs. 4-5 a kilo, while its wholesale price in the Middle East was in the range of Rs. 25-30, in the US it was Rs. 90, and in Europe it was Rs. 110. Even if investments were made for improvement of the product to make it marketable internationally which could double the prices in India, it would still leave a large gap to earn from in the global market. The trick was to get the produce right and get it acceptable in the markets around the world.

The Reliance Group feels that India possesses several positive traits which can make it globally competitive. It boosts of the largest arable land, has sunshine for a considerable time of the year, and has irrigation facilities in place. What Indian farmers need to do is to make their products traceable, and this is where the Reliance Group can play a big role. It will take up the processes of certification and verification. That is, get the produce, sort it and grade it for different markets, much like we see how an ordinary greengrocer does to fix different rates of the same product. Of course, this exercise will have to be taken up at a massive scale, and adequate decisions will have to be made whether to do this at the farmer's level or at the intermediary's level. This brings into consideration several factors, such as cost of acquisition, feasibility and certainty.

An important impediment that agricultural products face is their perishable nature. When it comes to grains (cereals and pulses), not much of problem is faced as they can last longer even when they are stored under ordinary conditions. On the other hand, vegetables and fruits need a perfect system because they can perish in a week's time if an adequate system (of refrigeration and transportation) is not devised. And when you are dealing at the international level, you need to set up a massive infrastructure for that. This is where distribution logistics are needed; and this will greatly add up to the farmer's income at the basic level. The difference in purchase and sale prices has been termed as 'arbitrage' by the Reliance. This arbitrage will do a lot of good to the Indians as did the IT industry. For example, the IT firms in the US needed to pay a very high price per man hour; but then they outsourced jobs in India and in the process paid less than what they paid in the US; but this gave a leverage to India as the IT sector in India saw a great boom; and with time, the Indian IT sector produced efficient professionals who made India an IT brand by itself. This has led to reduced arbitrage over time; that is, the US firms are paying Indians quite close to what they are paying in the US; and with time, this difference too will melt away. Today, India is a formidable IT brand in the world. The Reliance Group feels that if the same approach is adopted in the agricultural sector, it could lead to a similar outcome, at a much greater scale, because 60% of our manpower finds jobs in this sector. We can now hear of several cases in which young professionals are giving up their jobs to try their luck in the agricultural sector; the ideology that the Reliance developed has much to do with this development.

Employment is a sizeable problem in the world, and a large chunk of our youths need an opening in which they can prove their talent to enter the professional life, and nothing could be better than retailing for a majority of them. The Reliance Group feels this way because every young man in India cannot hope to become a doctor, engineer or manager, mainly owing to lack of education. Retailing opens a vast corridor for undergraduate manpower, many of them have attended only up to high school. There is need for this vast manpower to be engaged in some sensible jobs, and retailing throws up this opportunity. Even the organized sector has potential to absorb a large segment of this youthful manpower, leave alone the unorganized sector. The organized sector can employ as many as 1.5

million of them and give them a decent, dignified job, if they are utilized in retailing of the agricultural products.

The Reliance Group has put in infrastructure to study and understand the power structure at the village and tehsil levels and also ascertain the farmer's concerns. A farmer works on the field with his family, but all of the family members cannot be employed on the farm throughout the year, and in that sense, about 80% of the manpower remains unused. This is mainly because there are no buyers for the produce. The Reliance Group hopes to exploit this potential to raise the income levels while getting a higher output, because it will take up the responsibility for marketing the produce while the farmer takes responsibility for the produce; even in farming, the farmer will get assistance in the form of advice, scientific methods, implements, irrigation facilities, fertilizers and seeds.

Thus, the multidimensional approach propounded by the Reliance rests on reducing the cost of agricultural products to consumers to as much as 20%, increasing the efficiency of farmers helping them to earn 600-700% more than their present income levels in the next few years. And the Reliance hopes to achieve this mind-boggling goal by increasing the output. For example, the fresh produce can be doubled from the present 150 million tonnes to 300-400 million tonnes over a period of a few crop cycles. When quality is ensured, it is easy to win the customer's trust. So, as the Reliance understands it as a whole, that is, it is coordination of the yield-productivity-distribution story. Unlike other players, who enter the scene when the market has matured, the Reliance strategy is to develop the market.

The Reliance Group has shown it in other sectors that it can achieve this. It was laughed at when it said that they will get 10 million phone users, but they developed the market to the extent that all the phone operators have more than this share. The phone market has developed to the extent that several operators are able to get 1 million users every month. The Reliance Group foresees that the same story will be repeated in the agricultural sector, only it needs patient working. It has already put in pilot projects in several states, including Andhra Pradesh, Punjab and West Bengal, one in each region of the country to see the diverse problems faced by different regions. Today, Reliance Fresh, a part of the Reliance Retail, is doing well promising freshness and savings to the customers, while bringing prosperity to the farmers in its farm-to-fork model.

Mukesh has already sourced many Indian talents from the market abroad for the agri-business. He feels enthusiastic that the response of these professionals has been positive, especially in keeping with the fact that the saving element for them is at par which they are doing abroad. He gives an example. If a person is earning $ 1, 00,000 in the US but due to high cost of living is able to save about $ 15,000-20,000; if he is given an opportunity to work in the motherland with the same saving element, he would be better off, and this is what the Reliance hoped to do.

Mukesh sees a lot of promise in agriculture. He says that in the earlier times, people favored finance, then marketing, then engineering, and now the in-thing is agriculture, because its true potential has not been exhausted, and it is in this field that he hopes to do really well. This is a big change in the mindset, and is a welcome change. He says that the rural areas will have to be developed as a market coupled with raising their incomes. All these efforts have to be integrated and coordinated.

Reliance into Retailing

Mukesh knows it well how to make the most of the opportunities that come his way. He was already in businesses which helped him launch himself into retailing, and there is a big scope and can well be described as the business of the future. The Reliance group operates as many as 11,000 convenience stores, clothing outlets, jewellery showrooms and supermarkets, and also has plans to encompass in his embrace thousands more of outlets across towns with a view to empower and enrich them; and this would make the Reliance Group an unbeatable entity. While Walmart and Amazon plan to take on the Reliance, it would be virtually next to impossible to replicate what the Reliance has already achieved and the more that it intends to do in retailing. Another thing that favors Mukesh is that he operates in his own land, where he can operate without any restrictions which there would be aplenty for the foreign players. They have already suffered in 2018 when the Walmart had signed a deal to acquire Flipkart, which coincided with the government unveiling stringent new rules on online retail, forbidding foreign companies from selling their own inventory. As the competition gains intensity, there are chances that the Reliance would emerge a far stronger player to contend with.

Reliance and SEZs

Even 50 years after independence, towards the end of the millennium, India needed to buck up its industrial base as industrial development had not taken place to the optimal level. To achieve this purpose, the policy of SEZs was forged up. In fact, India was one of the first in Asia to recognize the effectiveness of the Export Processing Zone (EPZ) model in promoting exports, with Asia's first EPZ set up in Kandla in 1965. With a view to overcome the shortcomings experienced on account of the multiplicity of controls and clearances; absence of world-class infrastructure, and an unstable fiscal regime and with a view to attract larger foreign investments in India, the Special Economic Zones (SEZs) Policy was announced in April 2000. This policy intended to make SEZs an engine for economic growth supported by quality infrastructure complemented by an attractive fiscal package, both at the Centre and the State level, with the minimum possible regulations. SEZs in India functioned from 1.11.2000 to 09.02.2006 under the provisions of the Foreign Trade Policy and fiscal incentives were made effective through the provisions of relevant statutes.

The Special Economic Zones Act, 2005, was passed by Parliament in May 2005 which received Presidential assent on the 23rd of June, 2005. The main objectives of the SEZ Act included generation of additional economic activity; promotion of exports of goods and services; promotion of investment from domestic and foreign sources; creation of employment opportunities and development of infrastructure facilities. It was expected that this will trigger a large flow of foreign and domestic investment in SEZs, in infrastructure and productive capacity, leading to the generation of additional economic activity and creation of employment opportunities.

The SEZ rules provide for simplified procedures for development, operation and maintenance of the SEZs and for setting up units and conducting business in them; single window clearance for setting up of an SEZ or a unit in an SEZ concerning matters whether in the domain of the Central or State Governments; and simplified compliance procedures and documentation with an emphasis on self-certification.

The Reliance had become interested in the SEZ policy right from the beginning. For Mukesh, the logic of setting up an SEZ was simple that it was going to create millions of jobs as India was long on talent and there was need to create as many jobs in manufacturing and services as may be possible; and setting up SEZs materialized this idea into reality. From the earliest time from when the idea of setting up the SEZs was being mooted, the Reliance Group was out on survey; it found that the total land bank of India was around 750-800 million acres, out of which around 500 million acres could be potentially farmed, of which only about 300-350 million acres were being used for cultivation. That meant that there was another 150 million acre land which could be utilized for farming. Farming gives bread and butter to about 100 million households in India. The land which cannot be potentially farmed contains huge opportunities, as there is need to employ a large number of professionals (for example, about 8, 00,000 engineers being produced every year) and semi-professionals (for example, about 4-5, 00,000 being produced every year). If the idea of SEZs is brought into reality, there was a potential of introducing about 2 million youths of different categories into the workforce over the next 20 years; and to keep them meaningfully employed, there would be need to create jobs for them.

In the present scenario, there are not many jobs in the government sector, while in early 2000, the government was not doing much to provide adequate support for self-employment; in such a case, the onus for creating jobs fell on large companies like the Reliance, and which was ready to do this; because it had faith on the Indian talent, which needed to be nurtured, and there was a huge market within the country even if the market outside the country is not explored.

The SEZ policy gave an opportunity to create an integrated infrastructure; and if the government assured that this policy was going to be in practice for the next ten years, it could potentially change the employment and industrial development scene quite dramatically. The Reliance Group hoped to create such infrastructure in the SEZs which could attract foreign companies and investors, changing the financial sector quite effectively. The Reliance Group also studied the SEZ-like ideas which were being put into practice across the world, including those in Shanghai or Shenzen or Korea or Malayasia or Singapore.

The SEZs the Reliance Group aspired to build were to have all integrated facilities, like airport, seaport (if in coastal area), transportation, power and housing (for workers and others) and all these should come at a sensible and attractive price. So far as this concept was concerned, the Reliance Group was confident of competing with those of the best in the world maintaining global standards while being economic, together with a bank of talent. Mukesh had revealed in the early 2000s that he hoped to go for a number of SEZs across the country, so that the youths are given jobs.

Mukesh is apprehensive that the size of an SEZ matters much. If the infrastructure does not cater to the needs of a large area, the cost factor would go up, and this will put the entire project out of competition. He also feels optimistic about his agri-business and SEZ business, and says that they can be beneficial only in the long run, and that he has kept funds apart for these purposes. This will surely lead to show the promising brilliant sun to the world obliterating all gloom.

Facebook Deal with Reliance

In August 2019, Mukesh Ambani, while addressing the company's shareholders at the annual general meeting, said that the group has prepared a roadmap for becoming a zero net-debt company within the next 18 months. This deal with Facebook significantly contributes to realize the goal.

Facebook has entered a deal with the Reliance to invest Rs. 43,574 crore in the Jio Platforms, a unit of the RIL for a 9.99% stake. This will help the RIL to reduce debt and strengthen the company's social media presence in its largest market, especially for its WhatsApp unit. This transaction will value the Jio Platforms at Rs. 4.62 lakh crore. It is the parent of phone and data unit Reliance Jio Infocomm and various digital app platforms such as Jio-

Mart, Jio-Saavn, and JioCinema. By this deal, Facebook has earned a seat on the board of the Jio Platforms, along with that of an observer. However, this deal will not affect the status-quo of Jio and WhatsApp, and they will continue to function as independent units, and continue to stick to their own business models and will also collaborate in areas where they see synergies. The Jio Platforms, Reliance Retail and WhatsApp have also entered a commercial pact to cross-leverage ecommerce platform Jio-Mart and WhatsApp, to grow both businesses. The companies will work closely to enable the consumers to access the nearest kirana stores for delivery of products and services to their homes by seamless transaction as the Jio-Mart will make use of the WhatsApp. The main focus of the deal is to come up with digital-based solutions for 60 million micro, small and medium businesses, 120 million farmers, 30 million small merchants and millions of small and medium enterprises in the informal sector. Its focus is on creating new ways for people and businesses to operate more effectively in the growing digital economy.

A government official said that the deal could be subjected to close scrutiny by the anti-trust watchdog given both companies have the private data of millions of Indians, which could give the two undue advantage against rivals, including Amazon, Google and even the new startups. This coming together will have big impact as the Reliance Jio Infocomm has about 388 million users, Facebook has 328 million users while WhatsApp has close to 400 million users. This combine will make the entity unbeatable. And the most important thing about this point is that the Competition Commission of India has approved Facebook's investment in Jio Platforms for a 9.99% stake.

This stake will be owned by Jaadhu Holdings LLC, a wholly owned subsidiary of Facebook. This subsidiary was created by Facebook just the previous year.

This deal will help the Jio Platforms reduce its debt, which stands at about Rs. 40,000 crore. Of this deal, about Rs. 15,000 crore will be retained in the company and the balance will be used to redeem optionally convertible preference shares (OCPS) investments of the RIL in the Jio Platforms. With this, the net debt of the Jio Platforms will come down because of Rs. 15,000 crore cash which is being retained in the company.

This deal marks the formal entry of the Facebook entry into India's telecom sector; also it makes it one among the largest foreign investors in India's technology space.

On this occasion, Mukesh Ambani stated: "At the core of our partnership is the commitment that Mark Zuckerberg, founder of Facebook, and I share for the all-round digital transformation of India and for serving all Indians...In the post-corona era, I am confident of India's economic recovery and resurgence in the shortest period of time. The partnership will surely make an important contribution to this transformation."

Mark Zuckerberg stated: "This is especially important right now, because small businesses are the core of every economy and they need our support. India has more than 60 million small businesses and millions of people rely on them for jobs." He also added that the Facebook will play a role in getting the economy moving again.

This deal also helps Prime Minister Narendra Modi to realize his dream of 'Digital India' Mission which has two primary goals: (a) ease of living, and (b) ease of doing business, for every single category of individuals without any exceptions.

Other Deals

In addition to the deal with the Facebook, the RIL has also closed deals with four investors securing a total of Rs. 30,062 crore. These deals are with L Catterton (for Rs. 1,894 crore for a 0.39% stake), the Public Investment Fund (for Rs. 11,367 crore for a 2.32% stake), the Silver Lake (for Rs. 10,202.55 crore for a 2.08% stake) and with General Atlantic Singapore JP (for Rs. 6,598.38 crore for a 1.34% stake). Through these five deals, Mukesh has now sold a total of 25.09% stake in the Jio to 11 foreign investors amounting to a total of Rs. 1,17,588.45 crore. More such deals may also be seen in the near future.

Acquiring Businesses

Mukesh finds buying companies quite an easy stuff. It simply involves to go and sit in a hotel in the US and talk to investment bankers and buy all those companies which can be; but that doesn't give satisfaction. Despite this, he is not averse to acquiring businesses and companies, and over time he has shown that he can do this in style.

The RIL is in the process of acquiring many more businesses, and it has become almost a routine affair for Mukesh-led RIL. As I write this piece, the news is pouring in that it is in talks with the milk delivery platform Milkbasket and the online furniture brand Urban Ladder in order to strengthen its e-commerce play. It is also reportedly in talks with many other business such as the e-pharmacy player Netmeds and lingerie retailer Zivame, while it scripts consolidation with Future Retail. Over the past three years, the Reliance Group has invested heavily in different companies, which stands close to $ 3.1 billion (Rs. 23,300 crore). This investment has gone in such companies which are related to the main Reliance business to some extent, like those working in the field of telecom, internet, retail, digital, media, education, chemical and energy. While the Reliance Group has invested $ 5 million (Rs. 37.47 crore) in the Genesis Colours, it has put in a heavy investment of $ 603 million in Hathaway. According to an estimate by the Goldman Sachs, the Reliance Group has put in 80 percent of its investment in technology, media and entertainment, while its share of investment in retail is 13 percent, while it has put in 6 percent of capital in the energy sector.

The speed with which the Reliance Group is acquiring businesses and diversifying into different domains, the experts have come to contend that such an expansion approach will likely affect the future startups adversely.

Nurturing Talent

Mukesh sees a lot of promise in the young talent; he sees them raring to go, only they need opportunities, and he makes all possible avenues to create opportunities for them, whether it is in agriculture, commerce, manufacturing, power, telecommunication, petrochemicals or the like. When asked how difficult it is to motivate people to work their hearts out, he says that the youths are motivated by larger, higher goals and not by ordinary, day-to-day goals. He feels elated when he says that he has created opportunities for the talented youths from IIMs and IITs, and will continue with this process in the times to come.

Sensible Investment

The Reliance Group has made sensible investment in technology and in nurturing talent through developing skills. It relies on technology within and outside the organization to have things function without any hitch. Mukesh sees real future in technology, and says that it is a vital aspect of running a large business today; even a small business cannot thrive without technology today. It opens new avenues to people, at the same time, it has done wonders to transform the existing businesses and has made them exciting and easy, helping to make people perform more in the same time. Technology is all about saving time and energy, which amounts to saving money. Mukesh once gave an example why the Reliance went for helicopters to commute to the Patalganga project site which the people saw as the display of a flashy lifestyle; but for him, it was an essential part to save on time and energy, which could be made use of to do more things earning revenues. He describes these investments as 'facilitating ones'.

Mukesh is of the view that it is better to invest more in talents, infrastructure and quality of products than marketing. He feels it a part of his trait. In his words: "I believe that if my conviction is right, I will not need to go and explain myself to anyone. I believe that ultimately everybody will figure out what you are." This is the reason that Mukesh is averse to investing much in marketing, and he is quite true in his approach.

Reliance in Sports

The Reliance Group has also made forays into sports, and is also doing its bit to raise the sporting level in the country through its philanthropic arm, Reliance Foundation, chaired by Nita Ambani.

Reliance and Mumbai Indians. With a value of Rs. 47,500 crore, the IPL (Indian Premier League) is the biggest franchise-based cricket tournament in the world. And of the eight franchises, the Mumbai Indians is the most valuable franchise with a whopping value of Rs. 809 crore, in 2019, followed by the Chennai Kings, which is valued at Rs. 732 crore. The Mumbai Indians, one of the original 8 franchises of the IPL in 2008, is the most successful with four IPL titles and two Champions League Twenty20 wins. Its rights were acquired by the Reliance in 2008, under its subsidiary IndiaWin Sports Pvt Ltd. Nita Ambani represents the franchise in its team activities, and can be frequently seen in different matches.

The legendary Sachin Tendulkar was named the icon player of the franchise, he was also the captain. The franchise boosts of several iconic players from around the world. Interestingly, the theme song for the franchise is popular among fans: "Duniya hila denge." Also, after every boundary, the stadium disc jockey plays a fan-made song titled "Akkha Mumbai khelega."

Reliance and Football: The Reliance Group is expanding its wings in the sports arena. Now, it has made forays into the soccer field with an intention to create a new professional soccer league in India and lift the game's profile in the country. The Reliance Group has seen that now the Indians are taking soccer in a big way and the World Cups have done to lift its popularity in the country; the international soccer players have become household names, especially among the youths, and the Reliance Group seeks to exploit this opportunity and in the process, make the game still more popular and revenue-generating. In a survey, the Reliance found that the number of TV viewers has increased manifold over the decade, and this has made soccer the second most popular game in India.

It was in this view that Mukesh entered, in 2010, into a joint venture agreement with global sports marketing company IMG to promote sports and entertainment in India. The combined known as IMG Reliance made bid to acquire all commercial rights in football over the next 15 years from the AIFF (All India Football Federation), and these rights comprise sponsorship, advertising, broadcasting, merchandising, film, video and data, intellectual property, franchising and new league rights. It also comprises the branding and marketing of the Indian national team. It has planned to develop, popularize and promote the game from the grassroots to the highest level. The toughest challenge for the IMG, however, is to lift the Indian national team to the level of a global team, and with talented athletes in India, it was seen as a realistic goal for India to get a berth in the World Cup which, of course, is not going to be an easy task, given India's ranking, in the year 2010, at 142 in the world and at 23 in the Middle East (Asia Zone). In this venture, Nita Ambani is hopeful to make a meaningful contribution as she did in the IPL.

The JV will give grassroots support to the game through training and coaching facilities, along with upgradation of ground facilities. At a time, when the Indian corporates are hoping to buy the European teams, soccer has bright chances to grow in India.

Values

We have spoken about values that Mukesh and the Reliance have adhered to all along journey to the zenith. They call it 'growth through commitments', in which they make all possible efforts to care about quality, research and development, health, safety and environment, human resource development, energy conservation and corporate citizenship. They believe that any business can be ethical only when it rests on the nine core values of honesty, integrity, respect, fairness, purposefulness, trust, responsibility, citizenship and caring. The essence of these commitments is each employee conducts the company's business with integrity, in compliance with applicable laws, and in a manner that excludes considerations of personal advantage. The Reliance Group claims that they do not lose sight of these values under any circumstances, regardless of the goals they have to achieve. To them, the means are as important as the ends.

Mukesh and the Reliance Group have spoken of these core values time and again. In a recent talk to his employees, Mukesh states: "I want to share with you the most important lesson during this phenomenal journey which I have learnt from my father. The first lesson is courage. Sahas and Himmat zindagi mein bahut zaruri hote hain (Courage and resolve are very essential in life). Nobody has ever achieved in business or in any walk of life without courage, of course, whenever you do anything big, you do feel a little scared. Sahas ek aisi takat hai jisase dar ko bhi dar lagta hai (Courage is a power by which even fright is scared of). I want today's young leaders at Reliance to realize that achieving your potential is the quest of the ordinary; conquering the impossible is your destiny. The second lesson I have learnt is feeling empathy. Empathy means caring and sharing with every human being in our organization and the world at large. The more we care, the higher we grow as human beings. I understand empathy as dil ki baat (heart-to-heart talk), it is the wealth of your heart; the more you spend it on others, the wealthier you become. The third lesson I have learnt is to have absolute faith in technology and talent. In every business we have started, we have always embraced latest technology and have attracted the best talent. When top technology and talent work together, they produce unbeatable creativity, innovation and invention. The fourth lesson I have learnt is called something I call dil ka rishta (heart-to-heart relationship). Like my father, I value trust, loyalty and direct heart-to-heart relationship. Today you have a fabulous platform that will enable you to achieve multiples of what has been achieved by my generation."

Key Takeaways

- When Mukesh Ambani returned from the United States to assist his father with the Patalganga petrochemicals project, he began to eliminate the outdated board style that was unnecessary for the organisation.
- Mukesh preferred huge-scale offices among the largest on the planet for a variety of product offerings, including polyester, much like his father.
- Reliance came in and offered $5 million when its rivals were fighting with DuPont for innovation licencing in the range of $0.5 to $1 million.
- Since Mukesh expected the project's young designers to absorb the information quickly and experience a

quantum leap in their careers, he ensured they were distributed to it in large numbers.

- Under Mukesh's leadership, the organisation clearly leaned towards the United States.
- The organisation emphasises a global perspective while developing its talent pool by enlisting professionals among Indians living overseas.
- In order to help mistreated Indians obtain an MBA at the Wharton School of Business and return to their posts as RIL leaders, it had established a facility there.
- Mukesh emphasises the health of the organisation in addition to stressing Standard Operating Processes and Standard Operating Controls.
- The organisation has been consistently awarded for its health execution as well as security developments from these international foundations, local organisations including the Institute of Engineers, Indian Merchants' Chamber, and the Ministry of Petroleum.
- After work as its brand-new Jamnagar processing plant got underway, Mukesh Ambani's Reliance experienced an upsurge in excitement.
- This office was one of the most complicated places in the planet with a Nelson Intricacy Index of 14. Additionally, it included the largest alkylation machine in the world with permission from ExxonMobil.
- With the charging of Jamnagar-2, Reliance gained recognition as a company that had improved in task execution.

- To connect its designers in London, Houston, Frederick, Toronto, Shanghai, and New Delhi, Bechtel established a dedicated, specifically designed correspondence structure.
- The product frameworks had to be changed to enable seamless handoffs from all the key participants located in more advantageous locations across the world in order to integrate the subcontractors.
- In order to assist with work and keep up with the refining complex, Bechtel organised numerous RIL engineers at its offices. The firm had also ventured overseas since it constantly hunted for new oil and gas discoveries.
- Its portfolio included 13 blocks spread across six different countries, from Yemen to Peru, Australia, and Colombia.
- To access resources in the Marcellus Shale region, Dependence has agreed to a joint venture agreement with Atlas Energy, a US company.
- The organisation had carried out a few fruitful raids within the recognisable sphere of developing business sector nations in the region, including Indonesia and within East Africa (e.g., Kenya, Tanzania, and Uganda), but it had not established a marking project abroad.
- In its most notable month, Reliance Jio attracted 16 million customers, and in just one year, it attracted almost 130 million. This was the quickest supporter growth that any flexible communication organisation has ever posted.

- Reliance faced a difficult road ahead despite the envy of its business peers.
- The 30-year-old Akash Ambani was formerly a non-executive director at Reliance Jio Infocomm Ltd. After his father's resignation, he was named chairman the next day.
- As the owner of all Jio digital services brands, Mukesh Ambani will continue to serve as chairman of Jio Platforms Ltd.

❑

The Break Up

After their education, there was never a doubt that both Mukesh and Anil would join the family business. To start with, Mukesh worked in the capacity of manager of facilities, while Anil later joined as an executive dealing with government officials, investors and the press, because of his extrovert nature. These portfolios suited both, as Mukesh seldom appeared in public, while Anil liked to talk to people about the Reliance, often in his stylish expensive cars, at food joints across the city. The difference was evident even in their personalities too. Mukesh mostly dressed simple, while Anil liked to flaunt himself and socialize with people. Sometimes, he could be spotted with high society members, taking them for getaways in his personal jet. In marriage too, their tastes were apparent; Mukesh married the girl his family chose; on the other hand, Anil married Tina Munim, the actress; and it is also learnt that she was looked upon with disapproval initially.

In 1985, when Dhirubhai had suffered a paralytic attack, the Reliance Group found itself in rough waters, mainly because he was in complete command of all company operations, while Mukesh and Anil were still in the process of grasping things. And not long before the company had suffered the death of Rasikbhai. The two budding Ambani youths managed everything well enough through the value system that Dhirubhai had created and inculcated in them; moreover, he had recovered much in a few months' time to return to a state that he could guide his sons, if not work. He remained as the chairman of the group. However, in 2002, the company was going to suffer a major shock when Dhirubhai breathed his last.

The shock was massive, but the two brothers were already in command, and it was expected that they would sail through the situation successfully. They took over the company as its heads; perhaps they settled that the older will get a more important portfolio than the younger one, so Mukesh became the Reliance's chairman, while Anil its vice-chairman; and it was also the time that the company was going to execute its expansion plans. The same year, the company increased its dominance in the petrochemicals sector through its acquisition of the main private-sector rival: Indian Petrochemicals Corporation.

The company was not content with this; it also made a great diversification effort and targeted the telecommunication sector. As the company believed to invest in the business of the future, it went for the fast-growing cellular phone market. It was in the same year that the Reliance set up its own phone service—Reliance Infocomm.

This was during this phase that the relationship between the two brothers became strained, visibly over who had more power. Mukesh was unhappy with his brother when he announced a power-generation plant without having discussed it with him; and Anil was no less dissatisfied when Mukesh had restructured the entities that managed the family's Reliance shares without any intimation to him. Maybe, the attitude of the two had kicked off a heap of dust. While Mukesh took himself granted as the undisputed boss, Anil considered himself to be an equal partner in the entire business, though he functioned as the vice-chairman.

The matter took to a head when the Reliance board passed a motion that Anil henceforth would be 'under the overall authority of the chairman'. Naturally, Anil had to feel miffed about this, and this led to a sort of feud between two. In protest, he refused to sign the Reliance's financial statements describing them inadequate disclosures, and maybe at his behest, the directors of a subsidiary under him resigned to show solidarity with him. This bone of contention could affect India as the Reliance had become a prominent company, so even the union finance minister urged the two brothers to patch up.

In the end, a truce was brokered by the brothers' mother, who proposed a breakup of the Reliance Industries into two roughly equal components. Mukesh Ambani remained the head of the company's petroleum, petrochemical, and textiles operations, and Anil Ambani regrouped the company's telecommunications, energy, capital finance, and other operations into a new company. The breakup of the company took place in 2006. It was agreed that the two brothers would not become each other's competitors in the next 10 years.

As a result of this division, the Reliance Industries emerged as a focused and highly integrated petroleum and petrochemicals challenger to the global heavyweights.

On the other hand, the fortunes of Anil Ambani began to dwindle, mainly because his power business racked up huge debts and his telecommunication business witnessed cut-throat competition. In this competition, the two brothers too emerged out as competitors with each other. Actually, the division between the two brothers could be called equitable because so much was at stake. At the end of the division, Anil's net value stood at $ 45 billion, while Mukesh's net value stood higher by $ 4 billion. With this, the business acumen came into play. Anil now involved himself in projects he could have avoided for some time, such as film production, and spending money on non-essentials, such as screening of films at his expense.

In 2018, on the occasion of Akash's marriage, Anil was presenting himself at the gate welcoming the guests and performing the familial duties with aplomb, making sure that each guest was comfortable and refreshed, and was also taking time out to advise Akash how he could present himself suitably on the occasion, he was keeping hidden his emotions under check because he was just 10 days away from a deadline to repay $ 80 million debt, imposed by the court, which could result into his imprisonment even. He did not allow any strain of his dwindling business fortunes at this time when he was locked in negotiations with his brother Mukesh to bail him out this awkward situation. Mukesh bailed out his brother from a debt when his mother insisted on his help, and in this process, bought the assets of the Reliance Communications. Apparently, Mukesh had acted more like a businessman than an elder brother, when he sought the collateral; and he was quite right to do so, because this was not to be the end of financial trouble for his brother; there could be more to follow. Even in this deal, the family described the negotiation as 'amicable', which continued right until the deadline, yet there is reason to believe that this amicable deal could not have been carried out without some element of pressure at the behest of the elder one.

The problems for Anil are yet far from over. The State Bank of India is already making a bid for Anil's insolvency, and there may be tussle between different lenders, including the foreign ones, to grab his assets. A long legal battle seems to be a natural course for him. Let us wish him all the best, if he survives all these, and it would be better for him to ascertain where things started to go out of control and what he can do to bring things back on the track.

Despite its forays into the telecommunication sector, the main thrust of Mukesh-led Reliance Industries Ltd. remained on the petrochemicals and petroleum sectors. In 1999, the Government of India had auctioned off 25 blocks for exploration, inviting bids in the form of royalty percentage offers. The Reliance went all out for these and won 12 blocks in auction. It also promptly set up its own infrastructure and constituted expert teams, backed by the oilfield services by the Halliburton and Schlumberger. The

Reliance commitment and investment soon saw a positive outcome when it was able to explore and discover natural gas reserves estimated at some 14 trillion cubic feet, the largest natural gas field discovered in India in decades. This discovery was made in the Krishna-Godavari basin in the Bay of Bengal. The company struck again discovering another gas field in the Bay of Bengal, this time off the Odisha coast.

Enthused by its successful exploration efforts, the Reliance unveiled an ambitious expansion program for the second half of the 2000s. The company's plans included a $6 billion extension of the Jamnagar site, doubling it in size and making it the world's largest refinery by 2009. The company also announced that it intended to spend $10 billion on further oil exploration efforts, targeting the international market. In this way, the company hoped to increase its production tenfold by the end of the century. At the other end of the petroleum market, the company launched a $1.5 billion expansion of its Reliance gas station chain, with the goal of 6,000 stations. The company also expanded internationally, becoming the world's leading manufacturer of polyester yarn with the acquisition of Germany's Trevira. In addition, the company boosted its telecommunications wing, acquiring U.K.-based FLAG Telecom, an operator of a 50,000-kilometer underwater fiber-optic cable network.

Thus, we can see that the break-up between the two brothers has resulted in quite diverse outcomes. This absolutely proves that business flourishes when you have right approaches, strategies and talents, rather than wealth and extravaganza.

❑

Success Secrets

Author's Note

In the ever-evolving landscape of business and entrepreneurship, certain individuals stand out as beacons of inspiration, guiding others on the path to success. Mukesh Ambani, the visionary business magnate and the driving force behind Reliance Industries, is undeniably one such luminary. His journey from a transformative childhood to steering one of the largest conglomerates globally is a saga of determination, innovation, and unwavering principles.

"Success Principles of Mukesh Ambani" is a meticulous exploration of the life, principles, and achievements of this iconic figure. As we delve into the pages of this book, we embark on a chronological journey through the chapters of his life. From his formative years and education to the pivotal moments that shaped his destiny, we unravel the layers that make up the man behind the empire.

The narrative unfolds in three distinct sections, each offering a unique perspective on Mr. Ambani's life. We start by delving into the intricacies of his family background, childhood, and early education, providing a context for understanding the roots from which his principles have grown. The second section traces the continuous growth of Reliance Industries under his leadership, exploring the challenges faced and conquered along the way.

The heart of the book lies in the third section, where we distill his principles and learnings into ten key insights. These principles, ranging from having courage and self-belief to being empathetic and innovative, serve as guiding lights for aspiring entrepreneurs and business leaders. Through real-life examples and anecdotes, we illustrate how these principles have not only shaped his success but also hold universal relevance for those navigating the complexities of the business world.

In the final chapter, we synthesize the wealth of information presented, providing a comprehensive summary that encapsulates the essence of his success principles. As you turn the pages, we invite you to glean insights, draw inspiration, and apply these timeless principles to your own journey.

"Success Principles of Mukesh Ambani" is more than a biography; it is a roadmap for those who aspire to achieve greatness in the world of business. May this exploration of his life and principles serve as a source of motivation, wisdom, and empowerment for all who seek to carve their own path to success.

– Sujata Singh

❑

10 Success Principles of Mukesh Ambani

Every person have a set of beliefs and principles, which they made through their past learnings and lessons. Some of the principles come from their ancestors and some through the adversity of life. One of the wealthiest people in business in India is Mukesh Ambani, who serves as Chairman, President, and CEO of Reliance Industries Limited (RIL). He has established several cutting-edge business practices and frameworks that have enabled him to create one of the world's biggest telecom and energy empires.

After his father died, Ambani's conflict with his brothers caused them to divide the business. To become a rupee trillionaire, he expanded his petrochemical, gas, and oil businesses into an international conglomerate. The Success Story of Mukesh Ambani, the Business Model Game Changer in India, in Creating a Great

Leadership Legacy. One of the wealthiest persons in the world is Mukesh Ambani. Ambani enjoys a unique position as Reliance Industries Ltd.'s largest stakeholder, a company his father handed him. His businessman father, Dhirubhai Ambani, took the company public in 1977, but he didn't merely rely on his fortune. How did Mukesh Ambani become so wealthy, then? Well, the answer to that question is, through his learnings and lessons taught to him by his father as well as his life experience. Also, he is a man of principles, his firm belief in self, risk taking ability, the habit of serving a higher purpose and many other considerations made him the man he is today.

In particular, his business acumen and entrepreneurial instincts have helped him establish and grow Reliance Group into industries including telecoms, gas, oil, fertilisers, retail, and medicines. Additionally, he is recognised for transforming Indian business and generating millions of jobs, particularly in the manufacturing and service industries. Over the years, his dedication to innovation, constant focus on operational excellence, and unwavering customer focus have made Reliance Industries one of the world's most valuable private companies. Under his leadership, Reliance Industries has also become a global leader in sustainable development and responsible industrialisation. Mukesh Ambani has displayed many principles that can be applied in business. One such principle is his focus on innovation and operational excellence. By constantly resolving to innovate and improve his company, he has helped Reliance Industries to become one of the world's most successful businesses. Ambani is also dedicated to sustainability, an essential principle in today's economy. Some of his other principles are mentioned below.

1.1 Have Courage and Self-Belief

"I did chemical engineering because it was supposed to be the future."

–Mukesh Ambani

This simple line, or quote fits Mukesh Ambani's personality perfectly, he is courageous and has a strong belief in himself. He is sure about his decisions, and would do things that is effective in future. Mukesh Ambani knew his degree would come in handy, even though not many people believed in him back then, and were quite surprised to hear his decision to procure a graduation degree in chemical engineering. Ambani knew his niche, his interest, and the fact he was courageous enough to not let their opinion come in the way of his future. He always said that believe in yourself, even when everyone is saying you will not be able to do a certain thing, if you are confident enough you should try your best to pursue it. Courage and self-belief is a most important thing in an entrepreneur's life.

One among many other of his principles is to be courageous in every situation. An entrepreneur is a leading figure who should be courageous enough to take risks. Just like his father, Dhirubhai Ambani, Mukesh Ambani believes in being courageous and having the ability to take risks and believing in your decisions. Ambani learned this from his father, who was known for his risk-taking ability. Dhirubhai always believed that if you think it will work, you should have the courage to pursue it. Dhirubhai Ambani dared to launch Reliance Industries Ltd (RIL) with just Rs 7,000 crore in the capital in the 1960s when the Indian economy was on the verge of bankruptcy when he knew that he would not get the loans from banks because of political pressure when no foreign company wanted to invest in India at that time.

However, he still persisted and achieved success by investing an appreciable sum of money without getting any return on investment, something we Indians rarely understand. Ambani, in an interview, talks about being courageous and says as an entrepreneur, "the first lesson is courage. Nobody has ever achieved anything big in business or in any walk of life without courage. Of course, whenever you do anything big you do feel scared or apprehensive but you have got to conquer fear to discover the hidden hero within you. With courage, with self-belief and the can-do spirit, you can overcome any adversity."[1]

As an entrepreneur and person, Ambani believes in "self-belief" and a "can-do" spirit. While doing his interview with *MoneyLIFE,* a personal finance magazine, he mentioned how he decided to opt for chemical engineering instead of textile engineering even with Vimal's growing success in the industry. Ambani said, "Nobody asked me to do chemical engineering. I chose to study science and which college I would go to. By that time -- the early 70s - Vimal was a fairly successful textile brand. So everybody

---

1 https://www.cnbctv18.com/entrepreneurship/here-are-9-rules-to-success-from-indias-richest-man-mukesh-ambani-2508201.htm

expected me to do textile engineering. I shocked them by saying that I would go to IIT."[2]

His decision to choose chemical engineering came in handy later when Reliance Industry started its polyester business. Ambani always believed in self-belief and taking the risk; even after joining IIT in the beginning, he moved to UDCT (present-day ICT). "Since Inter-science results were announced after the IIT entrance, I joined IIT, Bombay. After the Inter-science results in a few weeks later, I left and joined the University Department of Chemical Technology (UDCT) along with my friends."[3] Again, the risk-taking adventurous ability must have come through his father; so many things could have gone wrong with his decision to change his college. However, without being afraid, he showed courage and self-belief. Not only this time but when Mukesh Ambani suggested having face-to-face conversations and meetings as people have in Western countries.

It was hard for him to bring that into action, yet with his undying courage and self-belief, he was determined to make it applicable for better results. The story of what is today known as Reliance Industries Ltd., or RIL, has its roots in the small town of Panipat (Haryana), where Mukesh Ambani's father, Dhirubhai Ambani, was born on March 22, 1930, to Gopal Bhai, a businessman who had set up a cement manufacturing company which was later called Reliance Cement Limited, at that time, it was a struggling venture of the family, but the future looked bright.

---

2 https://www.rediff.com/money/2007/jan/17inter.htm

3 Ibid.

During his talk with another leading figure of the twenty-first century, Mark Zuckerberg, Chief Executive officer of Facebook, commented on the topic of an entrepreneur being courageous and self-believing. Ambani said, "So you know, all of us believe that we have to believe in ourselves. And all of us know as entrepreneurs that we don't succeed at the first attempt, and self-belief comes to you when you fail. And self-belief increases your confidence when you succeed. So courage and self-belief is something that I always tell entrepreneurs, remember that it's important."[4]

In business, he believes there are times when an entrepreneur has to make decisions that would affect not only him but his company as well as the lives of every employee working there. He has been confident and courageous in taking firm decisions. And as Mukesh Ambani said, , anyone can overcome anything with "self-belief" and "can-do" spirit. Mukesh Ambani says that entrepreneurship is about taking risks and building companies from scratch that may fail or succeed quickly. Since failure itself suggests something positive, it takes fortitude to face situations where we must embrace failure as an unavoidable part of life. However, this does not mean that we should give up on hope or optimism. All business owners must develop the skills to deal with failures like these and come out stronger than before by using what they learned and not giving up.

4 https://www.deshgujarat.com/2020/12/15/mark-zuckerberg-and-mukesh-dhirubhai-ambani-converse-at-facebook-fuel-for-india-virtual-event/

1.2 First Find the Problem You Want to Solve

"Our childhood was different. I suppose when you are left on your own; you find your true potential."

– Mukesh Ambani

From childhood, Mukesh Ambani, and his siblings were to find their own ways and problems Dhirubhai never watched over their academic success, instead he insisted on their self-dependence. Mukesh Ambani, from this learnt that if you want to be successful and find your true potential then it is important to find your own problem. Even during his Bachelors he was taught the same principle through one of his teachers. If you are do the work you have to do then the result will be according to what others expect from you, but if you find your own problems and work that you are going to do then the result will be according to what you expect from yourself.

Mukesh Ambani always experienced the need to find problems before solutions. When pursuing his MBA, he was called back to India to work in the polyester plant that Dhirubhai Ambani planned to set up. After returning, he asked his father about his roles and job, but the answer by Dhirubhai Ambani made him speechless. Mukesh Ambani asked, "When I came from Stanford University. I asked what is going to be my job? What would I do?" To that Dhirubhai replied, "if you are in a job, you are a manager. If you are an entrepreneur, you will figure it out."[5] That was the beginning of Mukesh Ambani's career

5 https://www.businesstoday.in/latest/corporate/story/when-dhirubhai-told-mukesh-ambani-figure-out-what-you-want-to-do-71796-2017-02-16

as an entrepreneur, and he had no idea how much his future would change. Mukesh realised that he was not a manager. As Dhirubhai told him, when you get into the business, you should think like an entrepreneur who has to worry about the bottom line only: how much profit can he make out of this product? Dhirubhai Anand said, "You have to work 24 hours a day."

Mukesh Ambani also commented in one of his interviews, "My father said if you want to become an entrepreneur you will have to figure things out on your own. Only managers are told what is to be done, not entrepreneurs."[6]

As an entrepreneur, one must know what to do. You need to figure out what you are passionate about, your interest and your beliefs; that is the only way you will become successful. He further related one of the incidents of his life, when he was pursuing his graduation in chemical engineering from the University Department of Chemical Technology (UDCT) (present-day Institute of Chemical Technology (ICT)), his professor asked all the students to find problems and then the solution and that he would grade them on the quality of the problem chosen and how it was later solved.

Ambani also mentioned that he had a passion for designing things that would improve people's lives. He stated that if someone came up with an idea and wanted to develop it, they should go ahead without waiting for permission from any authority or company and get started immediately with their ideas.

---

6 https://yourstory.com/2020/02/mukesh-ambani-entrepreneur-reliance-inspiration-quotes/amp

Ambani in the interview said, "The second piece that I learned is that as an entrepreneur, it is very important to find a problem that you want to solve that you are passionate about. I was blessed to have Professor Sharma at the University Department of Chemical Technology (UDCT) (now Institute of Chemical Technology (ICT)).

He would always say, "I am not going to give you a list of problems and then you can go and work on anything, you find a problem and then I will grade you on the quality of the problem that you find and then I will grade you on the quality of solution that you actually do. So the same rules apply for an entrepreneur that it's not solving problems, it is first finding problems. Once you find the problem, then you solve it."[7]

For an entrepreneur, it is vital to know their interest and about their passion, and it is important to understand where you stand. What you want to do, what you expect from yourself, and all that can be determined by simply finding your own problem rather than asking others about the job you need to do. And who in life doesn't want to become successful on their own through something they love to do? So if the question arises today, who wants to become a successful entrepreneur? This would be very hard to answer in one word because many types of entrepreneurs exist. However, we can still say that most of us want to have a stable business or work for ourselves instead of working at someone else's company or just sitting in our boss' office and waiting for our salary (not saying this happens every day). So if you ask, the answer would be: 'Yes, most of us want to be successful entrepreneurs.'

---

7 https://www.cnbctv18.com/entrepreneurship/here-are-9-rules-to-success-from-indias-richest-man-mukesh-ambani-2508201.htm

Even in life, what others say matters, but to a limit. Your passion comes first because when you are interested in something, you will be able to reach your set goals and objectives through it. This principle of finding the problem first is one of the keys that made Reliance achieve its growth. The company started from a small-scale industry, and now most of the sectors have been incorporated under the name of Reliance Industries Limited (RIL). Today RIL has reached the position of one of the biggest companies in India and has become the largest oil and gas corporation in India, which holds more than 40 per cent of the market share of Indian Oil Corporation Ltd (IOCL), the country and owns the monopoly for producing electricity in the country through its state-owned power generation utility called NTPC. This is sufficient evidence that, as an entrepreneur, finding problems rather than asking what to solve will ultimately lead to success.

1.3. Trust Your Team as They are Your Biggest Power

"Relationship and trust are the bedrock of life."

– Mukesh Ambani

Trust and relationship, indeed both of them in some or the other way makes what you are, and what you are going to be. Yes it is important to have self-belief and confidence. And yes, it is important to find yourself, but what is more important is how you solve them. You can never create something out of scratch without trusting the people around you, who wish to do the best they can. Mukesh Ambani believes, "Identify your problem but give your power and energy to the solution." Ambani said what is most important in life is the power of your relationship with everyone in your company, this will lead you to success.

Mukesh Ambani, has always been a person who looks forward to working with his team and company. Ambani believes that trusting your team is necessary as they are your biggest power. Beginning with the construction of his first facility at Patalganga. As was noted in a previous chapter, he had the wisdom to include SOPs and SOCS. But what deserves mention is that he has successfully established Reliance with outstanding individuals leading the company. "You can't do anything without the right team. And it is very important to align the team passionately to your own passion," [8] Ambani observed.

While conversing with the Chief Executive Officer (CEO) of Facebook, Mark Zuckerberg, Ambani talks about the trust and power of the employees of its company, "I have learned from my father, is really the importance of relationship, trust, and loyalty. The whole of Reliance right now, with hundreds of thousands of people, is one big family. We're not related by birth, but we are really woven together by passion, purpose, and conviction. We have faith in one another. We are loyal to one another, to this large Reliance family. For us, it's always one for all, and all for one. And I hope that many people around the world can relate to this. That's what we believe at Reliance and for all of us at Reliance, he will still be the founder, if

8 https://economictimes.indiatimes.com/magazines/panache/entrepreneurs-take-heed-here-are-mukesh-ambanis-5-career-lessons/articleshow/57321703.cms

we follow his vision in terms of investing in businesses of the future."[9]

This trust is visible in his working habit, he has always looked for the most remarkable people and given them the independence to operate. He has used the expertise of the public sector and, where necessary, even foreigners to start his own businesses. The layout of Mukesh's Jio headquarters in Navi Mumbai, where he spends a few hours every Wednesday, is similar to that of an open workplace. The workplace operates as a flat organisation without any levels of management.

"This is a paradox, running contrary to Mukesh's usual practice of running the business in offices behind closed doors and under a strictly followed hierarchical structure in the refinery business. But this was done with the specific aim to attract and retain talent Mukesh also believed that Jio was a start-up, and hence, it should behave as one. Hence the switch over to an open office plan.

For example, his team at Jio is headed by expatriates, representing some of the most experienced people in the industry globally. In a newspaper article, it is said that over 15 per cent of the total 20,000 people working on Jio were expatriates working in key roles. These expatriates had been recruited from all over the world."[10]

Mukesh Ambani has been wise to recognise that if Reliance is to expand, he needs top-tier professionals. In order to place the appropriate individual in the proper role,

---

9 https://www.deshgujarat.com/2020/12/15/mark-zuckerberg-and-mukesh-dhirubhai-ambani-converse-at-facebook-fuel-for-india-virtual-event/

10 Agarwal, Rajiv. *Persevere and Prevail Like Mukesh Ambani* (Rupa Publications India Pvt Ltd) 2020 pp. 80.

he has recruited talent from all over the world. Ambani hasn't hesitated to hire across countries, boundaries, and geographic locations. He has relatives and friends in important positions, but they are also people who have repeatedly demonstrated their abilities and are on par with the world's top experts. Therefore, Mukesh has ensured that Reliance is led and run by highly qualified and capable individuals, which may be a contributing factor to Reliance's rapid growth. There is currently a widespread trend among the most influential entrepreneurs to employ and promote highly qualified individuals. Trusting your team is important as an entrepreneur; giving them the flexibility to work and listening to their opinions are the key principles. If you want to be a successful entrepreneur, then you need to start working on building trust with your employees, and in turn, they will do better work for you and help you build your business into something that you can be proud of.

One must understand that Trust is built over time, the first step in promoting trust is understanding that faith has to be built over time with each other person that you are dealing with; it's not something that you can demand from someone or trick people into thinking that you have trust and accountability built into your relationship with them. Mukesh Ambani always believed in the power of his team and have faith in his employees. Ambani is one of those entrepreneurs who would listen to the problems his team faced, and the solutions they would want to take. This is probably one of the main principles, as it has been proven from many instances that he always looks forward to work with his team and hear their opinion to have a better success rate.

1.4 Success Comes at a Price of Hard Work

"I don't think that ambition should not be in the dictionary of entrepreneurs. But our ambitions should be realistic."

– Mukesh Ambani

An entrepreneur should be ambitious, but they should also have the power and will to work hard to make their ambitions a reality. People say as an entrepreneur one must be aware of reality and think logically, however it is not the same for Mukesh Ambani, he believes a person can be imaginative and successful. Ambani said, "Logic will get you from A to B. Imagination will take you everywhere." Ambani believes that you can have dreams but what is important is making it a reality. Well, to make your ambitions, your dreams a reality a reality, you need to dedicate yourself to that and work hard to achieve your ambition. Ambani while talking about hard work said, "Even when I was in high school, I used to spend long hours at the office on weekends." His diligence is what makes him best out of the rest.

There is a famous saying that there are no shortcuts; in every field, there is the need for hard work. Even if you try to take shortcuts and get out of the way, you will most probably fail in your task. We tend to get lazy and procrastinate, which leads to looking for shortcuts that would help us reach our goals, but in all honesty, there are no shortcuts to success. Mukesh Ambani is probably one of the individuals who never thinks of taking shortcuts. Instead, he believes in working hard to find success at the end of the journey. He has always been known as a leader amongst leaders, his work ethic is just something to be admired by everyone who knows him well enough, and we can't even forget about his philanthropic side, which also makes us proud of being Indians. However, you can't deny that he has become a legend because of his entrepreneurial skills and his perseverance.

His father, Dhirubhai Ambani, would be another individual whose life story will serve the example behind Mukesh Ambani's principle. When Dhirubhai first went to Aden, he knew that at the end of the day, he must work very hard to reach his goals. He worked as a petrol pump attender and pursued many other jobs to start his own business. But it was not easy for him to do so because, in those days, the people who owned businesses mainly were Indians, Chinese and Malaysians. At the same time, the poor Gujarati businessmen had no way to compete with them, especially since they had more money than they could use to establish their own businesses or buy a shop or something similar to set up an auto-motor repair garage, even if they wanted to try it out first on their own before they made a significant investment into it. But Dhirubhai was a brave man who did not give up easily.

Similarly, Mukesh Ambani learned this habit of working hard from his father, making it a principle of his life. When Mukesh Ambani was first called back to India to work in the Polyester Plant, he had no prior knowledge about the plant or its plans. The company gave him basic training for two weeks, after which Mukesh Ambani started work with no experience whatsoever and was expected to learn everything on the job itself. Only after four years did he learn all about the various departments within Reliance Industries Limited (RIL).

However, he decided not to stop and work hard to reach his goals, and he decided that even if it was omething he had done before, his strong will and hard work would indeed present a result that he would be proud of. And sure enough, his hard work gave the best results; he was able to complete the project in less time than he was given. In 1983 when RIL took over Air India, the company was still a small one with only two-three thousand employees. Today, it has grown to become the third largest private sector enterprise in India, employing over 3 lakh people.

In an interview, while discussing how an entrepreneur must know to work hard, Mukesh Ambani said, "Put on your running shoes, but remember that personal and professional success is not a sprint but a marathon. We are lucky to be living in a dynamic world where anything is possible but it is important to remember there are no overnight successes, you will need to be dedicated, single-minded and there is no substitute for hard work. Also, remember that in this marathon of life is not a rat race, it is important to achieve our goals but not at any cost."[11]

When today's generation looks at the success Mukesh Ambani has achieved, they fail to notice the pain and hard work behind it. Anyone who is successful knows that success comes with a price of pain and hard work, and they are willing to pay for those moments when success comes into their lives; all the moments in between are nothing but mere failures in their eyes, even if they are the happiest people ever. If you are looking for instant success, then you can forget it because there will be no such thing as instant success, and this is something we have known

11 https://www.cnbctv18.com/entrepreneurship/here-are-9-rules-to-success-from-indias-richest-man-mukesh-ambani-2508201.htm

forever. It is not true to think that any of us wants to be on top from day one, and we know what happens when that happens. With changing time people are now more concerned about the result than the process, the learning. We must also keep in mind that even Mukesh Ambani says that one should be aware of the cost. It is true that success needs persistence and dedication but still one should know when to stop and accept the results.

1.5 Money is a By-Product of any Business

"The regulator's job is not to guarantee us a profit, however much we cry. The regulator's job is to first ensure that the country goes forward and then make sure that the consumer goes forward."

– Mukesh Ambani

According to Ambani, everyone should understand that a business should not only make money but should uplift the people and the country. Mukesh Ambani always believed that every business should serve a greater purpose. This was said to him by his father, Mukesh Ambani always said that his father, Dhirubhai Ambani, said that any business that is done solely for money would never work. He added that people must feel good about what they do and the only way you can do this is by doing something that benefits society at large in some way or the other and not just yourself or your family members alone, Ambani also said that his father told him that he was fortunate that he had a business like Reliance which served people's needs and therefore it would be better if he continued with that business instead of starting another one for himself.

And it is true according to Mukesh Ambani as "he did not consider money as important as resources." [12] To him, "money used as a resource gave his company some flexibility and enabled his company to take risks." [13] Ambani also spoke about the 'Reliance' brand which has been associated with his name since 1989 when he joined the Reliance Group and how it continues to be an essential part of his life and he does everything possible to ensure its longevity. Ambani also shared how he felt when he received the award and how the entire Reliance team were so happy on seeing their leader being honoured with such an award and how he felt when he saw his brother Anil getting recognised as well. Ambani added that Reliance's core values are Integrity, Empowerment and Accountability and it is these values which are used by all employees working across different businesses and sectors of the company.

Mukesh Ambani said that every business irrespective of its type, must serve a greater purpose. Ambani always believed contributing something in society, he calls money just a by-product of any business. It is not just the philanthropy part but there is also an equal importance to creating value for society as well as for investors in your company. In an interview when he was asked what money means to him, he replied that, "Money means nothing to me really. My father used to always tell me that if you start anything just to make money, then, in his own words, `you are a fool,' because

12 Agarwal, Rajiv. *Persevere and Prevail Like Mukesh Ambani* (Rupa Publications India Pvt Ltd) 2020, pp. 12

13 Ibid.

you will not be good at anything else and also not make money."[14]

Ambani, also said that he had seen the effect of doing good or exemplary deeds as a businessman and so it became a part of his life's mission to do good works as well as business in India and around the world as well as his vision to bring about changes in the country from its social infrastructure point of view with an aim to help poor people and empower them through various ways including education, healthcare, empowerment, etc., As per a Forbes magazine report, Mr Ambani's company has invested over $500m in developing solar energy, telecom services and other ventures that have helped transform lives across the globe.

Ambani says that this principle was originally of his father who always sought to give opportunities to others, and always did things that would give a societal purpose to the family business. His father also had a saying that if you have money, don't just keep it with you but share it with others. In another interview, while talking about his principles he gives an example of the Reliance Industry, he observed,

"My father (Dhirubhai Ambani) started RIL with $100. When I joined RIL in 1980, the market value of the company was $30 million or $40 million and in 30 years, the opportunities that were provided by this country has enabled us to create wealth for India.

My father was a staunch believer that any business that has the sole purpose of making money is not worth

14 https://www.zeebiz.com/companies/news-money-means-nothing-says-indias-richest-man-mukesh-ambani-13806

doing, it must serve a larger societal purpose. RIL raised all its money from capital markets and from individual small shareholders, so we have created a million millionaires just by investing in RIL out of ordinary Indians and that is the process of creating wealth for the country. Once you create opportunity wealth follows."[15]

Before the launch of Jio 4G, Ambani said that Jio would help many people and create a society with easy internet access. He added that the company would work with the government to provide connectivity in remote villages and ensure that all Indians have access to the internet as early as next year through this project, adding that the state-run telecoms firm BSNL can also be involved in the project to get more data points for this purpose. He added that Reliance Jio has partnered with a number of companies like Accenture, Cognizant, IBM, KPMG and Wipro, among others, to implement these projects in different states.

Mukesh Ambani believes that there is a give-and-take relationship in every situation and business. If you provide opportunities and look for a greater purpose than money, you will receive wealth automatically. During his speech he motivated youth saying that its their turn to do something that will contribute in society. An important point to note here is that the Ambani family was always driven by a passion to make money, which meant entrepreneurship, but it never meant running a business to make money– they wanted to build value, not cash.

15 https://www.cnbctv18.com/entrepreneurship/here-are-9-rules-to-success-from-indias-richest-man-mukesh-ambani-2508201.htm

1.6 Accepting Failure is The Way to Success

"Failure defeats losers, failure inspires winners"

– Mukesh Ambani

Mukesh Ambani has always believed that failure is part of success, and instead of getting upset over failures an entrepreneur, learns from it. Ambani said, "Success is walking from failure to failure with no loss of enthusiasm." Ambani believes that without failing one cannot find success in life, you must know that every step towards success is made from your failed attempts. A person who is most successful, is also a person failed the most. Even Ambani himself failed in every step towards his journey of success. He once quoted, "I am a big believer that whatever has gone lies in the past. You should only learn from it, and you should only look at the present and the future. That's been my father's philosophy and mine as well." Ambani said that one must learn to accept the past and learn from it. Because what is gone is gone, crying over your loss would not make you profits, for making profits you must understand your mistakes, should look forward towards the future. To make your future better, should work for it in your present. This should be the main principle for any business to look towards the future and work for it in the present while learning from your past.

Mukesh Ambani once said in an interview, "In every 10 things I have done I have failed six times. It needs optimism in our approach to succeed. It will take us a long way to meeting our potential in the country."[16] It is

16 https://www.cnbctv18.com/entrepreneurship/here-are-9-rules-to-success-from-indias-richest-man-mukesh-ambani-2508201.htm

probably one of the most followed principles, not just by Ambani but by many other entrepreneurs, who looks for success but knows how to accept failures. Mukesh Ambani has consistently argued that admitting failure should be one of the basic tenets of any entrepreneur. After reading about it several times, the conclusion can be stated that being an entrepreneur is a constant struggle between success and failure; we want to fail quickly so that we can succeed quickly. But we also need to learn from our failures to avoid making the same mistakes again in future projects and business ventures. Knowing how to make the most of a mistake when it occurs to you is crucial, especially for entrepreneurs who are building their businesses.

In an interview listing his principles, Mukesh Ambani affirmed, "Failures are normal. With all the success that one sees, people even in my own case don't see how many times I have failed before I succeed, they are just a step before you succeed. So never get disheartened by failures. Learn from them but never give up."[17] Mukesh Ambani believes that failure is a step towards success; it is a part of your journey. Ambani, who has led the group to spectacular success in India, said failure has a place in your life, too. He said he always learnt from his failures. In an interview with ET Now's Karthik Srinivasan, Mukesh Ambani, chairman and managing director of Reliance Industries Limited, talked about the lessons learned from his earlier attempts at entrepreneurship, how he got into the business when nobody else wanted him and why he is now one of the most successful entrepreneurs in the world.

17 Ibid.

Mukesh Ambani, accepted failure and started a different thing. He tried for three years to make a success of Reliance Industries Limited (RIL). In all, he spent Rs 300 crores on this project which was considered very risky at that time because there were no precedents to follow. It had to be built from scratch with technology not available anywhere else in the world then. Ambani went through some difficult times. However, he never gave up his dream of being a leader of this country one day.

Ambani is indeed an example for our young entrepreneurs. A billionaire and the chairman of Reliance Industries Limited, Mukesh Ambani, believes failure is a stepping stone towards success while speaking at the Forbes India Summit. Failure is a very important phase in life because if you look back in retrospect, without failure there can be no success. Instead of dreading failure, one must learn from it because it is the first step towards achievement.

Mukesh Ambani says, "If you are always 25th in the class of 50. for you to go to the top 5 is easier than if you were in the top 5 of the class. That is taking advantage of the situation and that is what this generation has."[18] Being an entrepreneur is difficult because you will fail much more frequently than the majority of people (including those who work in corporations). But if you can embrace failure and grow from your errors, you'll be more prepared to be successful in both business and life. All business owners seek to develop lasting value through their creation of items that endure, are beneficial to others, and

18 https://www.republicworld.com/india-news/economy/republic-summit-mukesh-ambani-on-his-optimism-for-india-data-entrepreneurship-and-challenges-in-conversation-with-arnab-goswami.html

are important to society as a whole. They don't just want to make money; they want to build items that last.

Ambani's mantra for success is "Expect the best. Prepare for the worst. Capitalize on what comes." He said that everyone, every entrepreneur should always be prepared to failure, but should aim for success and work on whatever the result comes out.

Failures are inevitable because no one can succeed on their first try. You must learn lessons from your mistakes and never give up if you want to achieve your goal. You will take a long time to succeed, but if you work hard enough, you can undoubtedly complete this mission. Everyone experiences failure at some point. Therefore, don't give up and keep working for your goals. You'll feel fantastic when you achieve something you've been working towards for a long time. Being able to develop and learn new things every single day is the most great part of being a human. Mukesh Ambani believes, "All of us, in a sense, struggle continuously all the time, because we never get what we want. The important thing which I've really learned is how do you not give up, because you never succeed in the first attempt." [19] You've probably failed at something in your life, but are you taking the time to learn from them? If not, you should own your mistakes and remember what Ambani said: "Failures are normal."

1.7 Be Innovative with The Environment

"I have turned into a big nature fan as well… I can afford it more today. These childhood influences have shaped me into what I am today."

– Mukesh Ambani

19 https://www.brainyquote.com/quotes/mukesh_ambani_581355

Mukesh Ambani said himself that he is a nature fan. He looks out for nature more now, as with his capital he is able to do more for the environment. Mukesh Ambani is one of those many people, who believes in taking care of nature is a way to success. If asked a question, what is success? What do you think will be the answer? Success does not mean cash, it does not mean recognition, what success is a dream you want to live, a reality of your imagination, it is more of doing something that you want to do, but at the same time it should be something more. Success should be a way you can inspire people, it is a way that will help society to become its better version. Environment has given so many things to us in every part of our life, it's time we pay back something to it. And it is a business rule to give back something in exchange for what you want. Your success does not only depend on how you work, it is also your way of life.

Mukesh Ambani has made his motive to go green, he planted trees used seawater and many more. "What may be a less-known fact is that the world's largest refining complex also has another feather in its cap. It is also the site of Asia's largest mango orchard, putting Reliance on the path to becoming India's largest mango exporter."[20] Still, the real question is the motivation or reason behind this. Law requires every refinery to keep a green buffer zone surrounding the facility. This is carried out to remove any contaminants that may have come from the refinery. As required by regulations, trees are typically cultivated within this green zone. Many other steel mills have a various blossoming and non-flowering trees surrounding

---

20 Agarwal, Rajiv. *Persevere and Prevail Like Mukesh Ambani* (Rupa Publications India Pvt Ltd) 2020 pp. 143.

the plant. This was a very common procedure done only for legal compliance.

However, Reliance, the company of Mukesh Ambani, which most shows creativity and innovation while also handling his business, had to approach this differently. This was also accomplished on a massive scale, with a 7,500-acre green belt surrounding the refinery in the customary Reliance fashion. It is green, proving Ambani's mantra "Go Green" to be true. The trees cultivated there either cannot flower or are not flowering trees at all, which was the only distinction.

Mukesh Ambani always find things that would benefit the environment, and suggests that others should do the same others should. His principle is to serve the bigger purpose, money is a want but environment is a necessity. To the Bloomberg at the Qatar Economic Forum, Ambani affirmed, "We have no option as a society, as a business but to really adopt a sustainable business model," [21] he continued "I think that's a prerequisite for every business to survive as we go forward." [22]

Over 100,000 mango trees that produce 110 different species of mangoes can be found in this green area. The green belt also grows other goods like guavas, pomegranates, oranges, and cashews. The fact that no tree is allowed to grow taller than 10 feet in this orchard makes it easier to maintain and harvest the fruit from the trees. Reliance has invested in a qualified team to ensure the orchard's excellent output.

---

21 https://timesofindia.indiatimes.com/business/india-business/companies-must-go-green-to-survive-mukesh-ambani/articleshow/83736093.cms

22 Ibid.

"The orchard grows Indian mango varieties such as Kesar, Alphonso, Ratna, Sindhu, Neelam and Amrapali, along with foreign species such as Tommy Atkins and Kent from Florida, and Lily. Keitt and Maya from Israel. The orchard is irrigated by wastewater and desalinated water from the refinery. More than half the output from the orchard is exported, and the balance is sold nationwide through the Reliance fresh grocery chain, a part of the Reliance Retail network. A Reliance spokesperson has said that the margins on the mangoes were higher than any other petroleum products manufactured by Reliance."
[23]

In a similar manner, the Jamnagar refinery desalinates seawater without using any water from public sources. It desalinates and uses saltwater. Seawater is desalinated to remove the salt, but this process requires a lot of energy. Additionally, the heat produced during several refining procedures provides the energy. Reliance utilises free energy so well, that was being wasted. Additionally, the green belt's trees are watered by effluent that has been processed.

"This attitude of looking at things from a different angle is what separates the winners from losers. We need to have the ability to perceive adversities in such a manner and consider how we can exploit these to our advantage. We will find that unless we do so, we will always have the competition beating us. One's ability to compete in markets is also the ability to think differently and to convert the current situation's disadvantages in our favour."[24]

---

23 Agarwal, Rajiv. *Persevere and Prevail Like Mukesh Ambani* (Rupa Publications India Pvt Ltd) 2020, pp.144-146

24 Ibid.

An entrepreneur, Seeking to make his future should understand that contributing to environment is necessary, not just for law but as a human being. We use our resources and even have exhausted some of them, we are in the condition of having an ecological breakdown not only in India but in the whole world. We read about the exploitation of environment done by us humans to make our life easier, and then we ignore it. However, it takes a second to close running tabs, half-a-minute to water a plant, and a minute or two to ask others not to do it as well. Mukesh Ambani with such an immense empire has time to look at the environment, and is trying to contribute through his various innovative ideas. It is high time that we all also, give our best to contribute and make others contribute as well.

1.8 Always Look at The Positive Side

"Profit or loss is not guaranteed. That depends on the consumer and depends on the product. That's a risk that business people take."

– Mukesh Ambani

Mukesh Ambani believes in being optimistic, he believes that nothing is guaranteed in this big world of business. Sometime you will make a profit and sometimes a loss, however, no matter what the result comes out, an entrepreneur will only try to look at its brighter side. Winston Churchill once said, "A pessimist sees the difficulty in every opportunity; an optimist sees the opportunity in every difficulty." This statement/quote is a perfect fit for entrepreneurs. Entrepreneurs should always be optimistic, as they are the ones making decisions in the company; they should be firm and should be able to take hard decisions.

According to *Psychology Today*, "optimism doesn't mean engaging in wishful or fantastic thinking. It's a way of looking at the world that gives more agency to the optimist as being at least partly responsible when life is going well. Optimists have healthier outlooks and tend to live longer than their more pessimistic counterparts; they also are less susceptible to the negative effects of illness, fatigue, and depression. However, an unrealistic belief that a person's future will be full of only positive events can lead them to take unnecessary risks, particularly with their health and finances."[25]

Mukesh Ambani is a highly optimistic person, he in an interview said, "An entrepreneur is always positive; he's an optimist. There are many cynics, several negative people around but an entrepreneur spreads the positive energy that's really what I have learnt."[26]

His belief is that an entrepreneur is a person who spreads positivity, in the midst of negative thoughts. An entrepreneur should know about the situation yet should be able to look at the positive side, they should find the brighter part of the most darkest situations. An optimistic entrepreneur, knows how to accept failure yet who rises again to pursue success. They are those who would never get upset over loss, but who finds the way out of the situation and builds profit.

---

25 https://www.psychologytoday.com/us/blog/the-science-behind-behavior/201610/4-ways-in-which-optimism-helps-entrepreneurs-succeed

26 https://www.cnbctv18.com/entrepreneurship/here-are-9-rules-to-success-from-indias-richest-man-mukesh-ambani-2508201.htm

Here Ambani adds more to it and continues saying that people will surely criticise you, they are the naysayers, who will force you to believe that this certain thing is not possible. There are many people who are going to belittle you or your organisation, yet as an entrepreneur, you must ignore them and stay positive. While talking about cynics, Ambani said, "Keep your headphones on, fill your ears and minds with melodies of optimism, turn out the critics and the cynics, the naysayers - people who say this cannot be done and treat them as noise cancellation. Dance to your own music and take some risks in life because it is often the risk taker who changes the course of history, who innovates, who creates something the world desperately needs and contributes to the well-being of millions of lives."[27]

Ambani suggests that there are a lot of people who would call you out and name you a fake. They would demotivate you and make you doubt your every decision. However, it would be best if you do not listen to them. He says to fill your ears with "melodies of optimism" and go on and take a risk. According to Ambani, everyone has been criticised once in life. Still, instead of accepting and thinking about such negative criticism, an entrepreneur should take a risk and create things that will somehow help millions of people.

Mukesh Ambani, while giving an interview to Republic TV's Editor-In-Chief Arnab Goswami, said, "Reliance was around a million dollars in size when I joined. We have been a perpetual startup. I can realise what an entrepreneur goes through. This country should produce 100s not 1000s

---

27 Ibid.

of Dhirubhais (reference to his late father and founder of Reliance).

He used to say, what we can learn from others - *Agar soch badloge toh kismat badlegi*, If you change your mindset you will change your fortune. I feel younger when I am around 30-year-olds.

We have to understand that we are entering an era. We have grown up in a linear era. In that, we grow up by 1-2-3 steps. In an exponential era, we go from 1- 2 to 10 steps, so it is a propitious time for India to embrace these technologies and embrace the power of the youth. I see a new mindset and power of youth and also numerous problems. An entrepreneur finds a big problem and solves it.

Western friends say India is a country with a million problems. I say India is a country of a billion opportunies. And these opportunities can be seen. And that is the reason for my optimism.

Let's not forget that in 1991 we were at $350 billion (size of economy) now we are nearing $3 trillion. To get there in two decades is a long shot but we got there."[28]

If you want to be an entrepreneur, focus on the accurate facts, and eliminate your natural negative ideas for more upbeat, realistic ones. Develop the mental attitude that you can influence positive outcomes in your life. Make it a habit to tell yourself what you can do specifically to achieve. Get rid of the negative mindset: It's simple to become

28 https://www.republicworld.com/india-news/economy/republic-summit-mukesh-ambani-on-his-optimism-for-india-data-entrepreneurship-and-challenges-in-conversation-with-arnab-goswami.html

caught up in a negative thought cycle. Do something to stop that mental process. Pick up your favourite book, go for a walk, or turn on some music. Optimists can steer clear of some of these problems by upholding a healthy, realistic approach to optimism. The objective should be to attempt to see the positive side while still realising the challenges of the circumstance, as opposed to concentrating simply on "keeping optimistic" and disregarding other feelings.

1.9 Have Faith in the Next Generation

"At Reliance, we have always believed in investing in the business of the future and in investing in talent."

– Mukesh Ambani

Mukesh Ambani has been saying that believing in the future generation is essential in today's world. He motivates everyone to create a structure for the company that will outlast the leaders. He repeatedly emphasised that organisations are immaterial and bigger than the individuals who make them. He emphasised the need to have faith in the generation coming up to carry on the tradition with fresh perspectives, ideas, and energy. Ambani himself has created a system where the future generation can take it to a different height.

Mukesh Ambani, while delivering a speech on the occasion of Reliance family day, on December 28, 2021, which is the birth date of his father, Dhirubhai Ambani, he said, "All seniors -- myself included -- should now yield to the highly competent, extremely committed, and up-and-coming young leadership talent at Reliance."[29] He

29 https://www.businesstoday.in/latest/corporate/story/mukesh-ambani-talks-of-leadership-transition-at-ril-wants-to-accelerate-the-process-317120-2021-12-28

continued, "We should guide them, enable them, encourage them and empower them... and sit back and applaud as they perform better than us."[30] He ended without further elaboration. He saying that now is the time for all the senior staff, himself included, to sit back and appreciate the next generation for their performance. He says that it is crucial for any organisation to have faith in its future generation, that they will do even better than the current one. And if they fail to do so, it is the responsibility of the previous generation to guide them and show them the way to success.

He believes in learning from the new generation, as the current world, the way the current generation thinks because, with time, everything must change and update. Even the apps on your phones change with time and continuously update themselves, so why don't human beings? Ambani supports future generations and also tries to learn from them. Mukesh Ambani has credited his children with inspiring him to start an online business.

Mukesh went on to say, "My son Akash said, 'Dad, your generation doesn't get it. In the old world, telecom was a voice-and you only made money when one person calls and the other answers. In our new world, everything is digital. We can do a lot more with a digital network than just talk.' Isha and Akash belong to India's young generation that is far more creative, far more ambitious and far more impatient to become the best in the world. These young Indians convinced me that broadband Internet is the defining technology of our age and India cannot be left behind."[31]

---

30 Ibid.

31 Agarwal, Rajiv. *Persevere and Prevail Like Mukesh Ambani* (Rupa Publications India Pvt Ltd) 2020, pp. 149-150.

The fact that Mukesh did invest approximately $35 billion into Jio, enabling it to enter the mobile phone sector and rise to the top four companies by offering free voice call services and fast broadband speeds at incredibly low prices, makes his statements appear prophetic. After that, Jio Fibre was able to connect homes and businesses with fibre-optic connections in order to supply content and the Internet at quick speeds and at affordable pricing.

Mukesh Ambani has commented on this repeatedly, even while giving an interview to Republic TV's Editor-In-Chief Arnab Goswami, said, "The power of entrepreneurs is the ability to solve a problem and scale it. I have the largest faith in our young people in Jio. Data in the world costs 8-10 dollars per GB. When we set out to be an only data network as data is the foundation of the new world. If we did not have data in this era we will be left behind. We wanted quality and affordability.

We wanted to build something that every last Indian can afford. Today, we have the highest quality data for half a dollar for a GB. We have 25,000 engineers who made it possible. This connectivity, in a few years, will be ready to go to the world.

It is idea and innovation that will lead the world and not capital. Capital will be abundant for the right people today. I think we should really believe in the power of ideas and opportunity and they will win the hearts of Indians and the world for us.

What you have to do is make sure we open all opportunities to entrepreneurs To gather in boardrooms is different than what is happening in real India. I have met amazing start-up teams who will do something amazing in the next 36 months.

We have connected 1-9 millions schools, we have revolutionised the connectivity. In reality, things are happening much faster than what we are able to perceive. Just like Jio came out of nowhere. In two years we made it what it is today.

A lot of silent work is happening on the ground by unknown entrepreneurs which surprise you. You will see it too."[32]

Here, Ambani, shows his faith in the younger generations, he maintains that he has faith in the young people in Jio. He said we need to create opportunities for the young generation, should show faith in them. He applauds them saying the he met the best startup team, that will work for the better future. It is time for every business person, to now hand over their business to the future generation, so that they can work better not only for the company, but for the country and its people. It is time for everyone to create opportunities for the upcoming generations. To provide them a place to showcase their talents. It is time to believe in the start-up of the new era. Standing by his own words, Mukesh Ambani resigned and on June 28, 2022, made his son, Akash Ambani, the chairman of Reliance Jio.

Given that the younger generation is leading activities in the digital sphere and that they are also the biggest

---

32 https://www.republicworld.com/india-news/economy/republic-summit-mukesh-ambani-on-his-optimism-for-india-data-entrepreneurship-and-challenges-in-conversation-with-arnab-goswami.html

consumers of digital material, the future for Jio appears to be promising. These people are "digital natives," members of a generation that was raised in a world with constant digital input. Therefore, they will serve as the ideal mentors in determining the company's future course.

1.10 Be Empathetic and Look Out for Your Customers

"By empathy, I mean, put yourself in the others' shoes, and make sure that how you make them feel is how you would want to feel,"

– Mukesh Ambani

One of Mukesh Ambani's core principles is to 'be empathetic'. He believes that every entrepreneur should feel empathy. They should try and put themselves in others' shoes and think from another perspective. Mukesh Ambani explains empathy, "Empathy means caring and sharing with every human being in our organisation and the world at large, the more we care the higher we grow as human beings. I understand empathy as 'Dil Ki Daulat', it is the wealth of your heart, the more you spend it on others the more wealthy you become" [33]

Mukesh Ambani, while delivering a speech on the occasion of Reliance family day, on December 28, 2021, which is the birth date of his father, Dhirubhai Ambani, said, "We must be forever EMPATHETIC and COMPASSIONATE in our behaviour. We must be forever

33 https://www.republicworld.com/india-news/economy/republic-summit-mukesh-ambani-on-his-optimism-for-india-data-entrepreneurship-and-challenges-in-conversation-with-arnab-goswami.html

POSITIVE in our thoughts and action. We must be forever HOPEFUL about the future. We must forever follow the HIGHEST STANDARDS OF HONESTY and INTEGRITY. We must be forever INNOVATIVE and be forever ready to TAKE BOLD INITIATIVES in today's fast-changing world. As Reliance grows bigger and becomes more global, we must be even more committed to these guiding values and principles."[34]

The critical point Mukesh Ambani said was always to remember the company's motto, "We Care." This fundamental guiding principle had to serve as the organisation's foundation and be consistently reinforced, emphasised, and disseminated in all venues. He reaffirmed that all stakeholders, including shareholders, financiers, investors, workers, partners, and society, were included in the "We Care" concept. Mukesh Ambani is always attempting to make the best products but at an affordable price; he looks out for his customers and their need. He tries to see what his customers want from him.

"Mukesh Ambani had been inspired by the lowest-cost form of communication, the humble postcard costing 40 paise, to set the price of a call, when he had first launched the Monsoon Hungama offer, in July 2003 in the days of Reliance Infocomm. This was the precursor to his next step, to bring 4G smartphone prices to affordable levels."[35] He realised that most of the smartphones and other electronics were either from China or too costly to buy.

---

34 https://www.cnbctv18.com/business/reliance-family-day-2021-the-full-text-of-mukesh-ambanis-speech-11956252.htm

35 Agarwal, Rajiv. *Persevere and Prevail Like Mukesh Ambani* (Rupa Publications India Pvt Ltd) 2020, pp. 164-166.

"Jio then realized that the 24,000 price tag was too high for new phones and it had to find some other way. So the design team came up with the Jio Phone at an even lower price! They worked on the lowest possible experience that the users would need and they designed the phone keeping this in mind. This helped bring the prices down to feature-phone levels. This move also led to many competitors in the form of network operators bundling low-cost smartphones from companies such as Micromax, Karbonn, Intex and Lava with services that caused the data industry to be severely disrupted."[36]

The information above demonstrates how deeply Mukesh Ambani has studied his audience. He provides a product that meets their wants since he is aware of their needs and the price ranges at which they will be able to purchase it. If his audience rejected the provided item, he declined to receive it. Instead, he took action to create goods that suited his needs, giving him an edge over his competitors.

Key Takeaways

- Mukesh Ambani, Chairman, President, and CEO of Reliance Industries Limited, is among the wealthiest businesspeople in India (RIL).
- Reliance Industries is one of the most valuable private firms in the world thanks to his unrelenting commitment to customer satisfaction, consistent focus on operational excellence, and commitment to innovation over the years.

36 Ibid.

- Many business-relevant principles have been demonstrated by Mukesh Ambani. Some of his principles are:
  - Have Courage and Self-Belief
  - First Find the Problem You Want to Solve
  - Trust Your Team As They Are Your Biggest Power
  - Success Comes At A Price of Hard Work
  - Money is a By-Product of Any Business
  - Accepting Failure is the Way to Success
  - Be Innovative With the Environment
  - Always Look at the Positive Side
  - Have Faith in the Next Generation
  - Be Empathetic and Look Out for Your Customers

❑

Summary

To conclude or summarise everything that this book has been trying to say, Mukesh Ambani, as an entrepreneur, is a hardworking and a humble person. A perfect role model for entrepreneurs attempting to start their own business and firm. His management skills, as well as his ability to make the right decisions, make him different from every businessman. His principles are the main reason he can sustain longer. Ambani's principles are a result of learnings he received from his father, life experiences, and mindset.

It appears from Mukesh's business practises and approaches that he is continuing his father Dhirubhai Hirachand Ambani's legacy, upholding his goals and setting a good example for his offspring. The son of a wealthy, noble family received from his father's discipline, tenacity, and a nationalist attitude while receiving these traits from his mother, Kokilaben Ambani, to whom he was the most emotionally attached of all the family members.

Mukesh Dhirubhai Ambani, born on April 19, 1957, is a business tycoon and the wealthiest man in Asia. As of 2022, He started Reliance's backward integration process, moving the company upstream into oil and gas exploration and production, from textiles to polyester fibres, then onto petrochemicals and petroleum refining. Mukesh Ambani was born in the British colony, Colony of Aden, which is now a part of South Yemen. His father, Dhirubhai Ambani, decided to leave Yemen as it was now independent and risky for any outsider.

Mukesh's father never looked for marks and school but always asked him to gain as much practical knowledge as possible. Ambani studied chemical engineering at the Institute for Chemical Technology (then named UDCT), Matunga and graduated in Chemical Engineering in 1979. He also prepared for the civil service exams. However, he changed his mind and decided to pursue a management background at a renowned university. Ambani went to Stanford University in 1980 to pursue his MBA degree but returned to India when his father asked him to come back to start the Polyester plant.

Mukesh Ambani cofounded Reliance Industries with his father, Dhirubhai Ambani, in 1977. As the eldest son, he was supposed to work from 17 and help his father share the load of business. Mukesh needed to advance rapidly since he had scarcely any operational experience, notwithstanding his certificate in Chemical Engineering. He demanded taking on proficient norms and guaranteed that each newcomer was expertly qualified, experienced, and verified. Mukesh Ambani's father, Dhirubhai Ambani, worked on the Patalganga project, which was completed in a year and a half. He demanded close, personal interchanges and gatherings inside the venture group, which directly covered all workers for hire. Mukesh did not necessarily vote for granting agreements to organisations that bid the lowest. In an interview with Simi Garewal, Mukesh Ambani talks about the incident when Dhirubhai Ambani suffered from his first stroke.

He also recalls how instead of asking what happened to him, he tried to reassure Mukesh that he was fine and would make it. Dhirubhai Ambani died without leaving any will or dividing assets, so his elder son Mukesh Ambani became chairman and managing director of Reliance Industries Ltd. His younger son Anil Ambani was made vice-chairman. The lack of a will created a rift between the Ambani brothers, and it took the form of a significant dispute between them in 2004.

According to Forbes, Reliance Industries' market cap, as of 2022, is $228.6 billion. Mukesh Ambani left his imprint on RIL's set of experiences right off the bat. Our motto, 'Growth is Life', aptly captures the ever-evolving spirit of Reliance. Dependence had consistently preferred enormous-scale offices, a large portion of them surpassing the complete introduced limit in India and exceeding anticipated home interest. Mukesh had reproduced an outward engaged culture, depending on worldwide business sectors as opposed to protected markets at home. For instance, when its contenders were haggling with DuPont for innovation licenses in the scope of $0.5 to $1 million, Reliance stepped in and offered $5 million since they felt it would merit the potential chance to work with the best organisation in the world. Under

Mukesh Ambani, H.R. had a command to fabricate a top-notch association that would draw in a more youthful labour force and support and foster ability with an eye on development. The organisation had stressed a worldwide view by drawing in experts among the Indians abroad who needed to get back old pros from driving rivals in the US and Europe and the cream from India's high designing schools.

It had laid out an establishment at the Wharton School of Business to assist oppressed Indians with procuring an MBA there and return to join the positions of RIL chiefs. Under Mukesh's stewardship, the organisation had assimilated much of its initial security culture from any semblance of Bechtel and DuPont, RIL accomplices on different drives. The annual reports likened to those given by worldwide organisations offered data on RIL execution along essential components of word-related security, preparing and improving its representatives, social responsibilities, and ecological presentation history. Revealing rules by worldwide bodies, such as the well-being principles of the British Council of Safety and the American Society of it, were taken on to Train and Development.

Mukesh Ambani's Reliance was riding an influx of rapture after tasks were initiated at its new Jamnagar processing plant. With a Nelson Intricacy Index of 14, this office was among the most complex on the planet, equipped for handling probably the most tested sharp crudes. It additionally incorporated the world's most enormous alkylation unit under permit from ExxonMobil, permitting it to refine fuel that could satisfy Euro-IV guidelines. The Jamnagar Refinery Complex called for more than 10 million hours of configuration work, 4,000,000 cubic meters of concrete, 18,000 kms of electrical cabling, and north of 250 kms of streets alone. Bechtel set up a committed, exclusively constructed correspondence organisation to interface its designers in London, Houston, Fredrick, Toronto, Shanghai, and New Delhi. When the unit was charged in late 2009, Solomon Associates, the worldwide refining benchmarking organisation, put it in the top quartile of all treatment facilities regarding capital and working efficiencies. Dependence had consented to a joint endeavour arrangement with Atlas Energy, a US organisation, to get to resources in the Marcellus Shale area situated in the north-eastern US It expected that this arrangement would offer admittance to asset potential assessed at 13.3 tcf. The organisation had likewise wandered abroad as it is continually looking for new revelations of oil and gas. Its portfolio contained 13 blocks in six nations, from Yemen to Peru, Australia, and Colombia. The globalisation of RIL, apparently the following skyline for the organisation, looked questionable. Its obtaining Trevira, the German polyester maker, brought about a rushed exit in only five years. It then bid to procure Lyondell Basell, the Dutch refining and synthetic substances organisation, for $14.5 billion. Given the inadequate record of fruitful globalisation, it still needed to be worked out if the attractive benefits that Reliance had based upon in India could be moved to unfamiliar business sectors with equivalent achievement.

In late 2016, the organisation launched Reliance Jio, a versatile communication and broadcast communications organisation. It pulled in 16 million clients in its most memorable month and around 130 million in only one year. This raid will undoubtedly absorb huge capital assets and administrative transfer speed despite the fact that the jealousy of its corporate friend, Reliance, had a brutal street ahead. Akash Ambani, 30, was appointed chairman of the board at Reliance Jio on June 28, 2022. Mukesh Ambani had hinted last year that his children would assume more responsibility. He wed Shloka Mehta in March 2019. The couple welcomed a child in 2020, who was later given the name Prithvi.

One of the wealthiest persons in the world is Mukesh Ambani, who serves as Chairman, President, and CEO of Reliance Industries Limited (RIL). He has established several cutting-edge business practices and frameworks that have enabled him to create one of the world's biggest telecom and energy empires. To become a rupee trillionaire, he expanded his petrochemical, gas, and oil businesses into an international conglomerate. His businessman father took the company public in 1977 but didn't merely rely on his fortune. His business acumen and entrepreneurial instincts have helped him establish and grow Reliance Group into industries including telecoms, gas, oil, fertilisers, retail, and medicines.

Over the years, his dedication to innovation, constant focus on operational excellence, and unwavering customer focus have made Reliance Industries one of the world's most valuable private companies. He is also dedicated to sustainability, an essential principle in today's economy.

Have Courage and Self-Belief

Ambani believes in being courageous and having the ability to take risks. He learned this from his father, Dhirubhai Ambani, who was known for his risk-taking ability.

Courage and self-belief is the most essential thing in an entrepreneur's life. Ambani chose chemical engineering instead of textile engineering. However, he still persisted and achieved success by investing considerable money without any return on investment. Ambani believes in "self-belief" and a "can-do" spirit as an entrepreneur and person. Dhirubhai Ambani says that entrepreneurship is about taking risks and building companies from scratch. Since failure suggests something positive, it takes fortitude to face situations where we must embrace failure. Mukesh Ambani believes anyone can overcome anything with self-belief and a "can-do" spirit.

First Find the Problem You Want to Solve

Dhirubhai Ambani always taught his children to find their problems and solutions. As an entrepreneur, Mukesh had no idea how much his future would change when he started. As an entrepreneur, one must know what to do. You need to figure out what you are passionate about, your interest and your beliefs; that is the only way you will become successful. Ambani also mentioned that he was passionate about designing things that would improve people's lives. For an entrepreneur, it is vital to know their interest and their passion. Finding your problem can determine what you want to do and what you expect from yourself. This principle of finding the problem first is one of the keys that made Reliance achieve its growth.

Trust Your Team as They are Your Biggest Power

Ambani believes that trusting your team is necessary as they are your biggest power. The whole of Reliance right now, with hundreds and thousands of people, is one big family. We are not related by birth, but we are really woven together by passion, purpose, and conviction. Mukesh Ambani has always looked for the most remarkable people and given them the independence to operate. He has used the expertise of the public sector and, where necessary, even foreigners to start his own businesses. The layout of Mukesh's Jio headquarters is similar to that of an open workplace. Mukesh Ambani always believed in the power of a team and had faith in his employees. He has ensured that Reliance is led and run by highly qualified and capable individuals. There is a widespread trend among the most influential entrepreneurs to employ and promote highly competent individuals.

Success Comes at a Price of Hard Work

There are no shortcuts to success; there must be hard work, commitment and dedication. He has always been known as a leader amongst leaders; his work ethic is something to be admired by everyone who knows him well enough. Dhirubhai Ambani worked as a petrol pump attender and pursued many other jobs to start his own business. When Mukesh Ambani was called back to India to work in the Polyester Plant, he had no prior knowledge about the plant or its plans. Mukesh Ambani says that success comes with a price of pain and hard work. There are no overnight successes. You need to be dedicated, single-minded and diligent. He says personal and professional success is not a sprint but a marathon.

Money is a By-Product of Any Business

Mukesh Ambani believes that every business should serve a greater purpose. His father, Dhirubhai Ambani, always said that any business done solely for money would never work. Ambani also spoke about the 'Reliance' brand, which has been associated with his name since 1989. Mukesh Ambani believes that money is just a by-product of doing good deeds. His Reliance Industry has invested over $500m in developing solar energy, telecom services and other ventures. Ambani's father, Dhirubhai Ambani, started RIL with $100. Ambani said that Jio would help many people and create a society with easy internet access. Jio has partnered with several companies like Accenture, Cognizant, IBM, KPMG and Wipro. Ambani believes that there is a give-and-take relationship in every situation and business.

Accepting Failure is the Way to Success

Ambani believes that without failure, one cannot find success in life. Every step towards success is made from your failed attempts. Being an entrepreneur is a constant struggle between success and failure. We want to fail quickly so that we can succeed quickly but also learn from our mistakes. Mukesh Ambani believes that failure is a stepping stone towards success. He said he always learnt from his failures and never gave up on his dream. Ambani is the chairman of Reliance Industries Limited (RIL), India's biggest private sector conglomerate. Mukesh Ambani's mantra for success is to expect the best. Prepare for the worst. Capitalise on what comes. Entrepreneurs seek to develop lasting value by creating enduring items that are beneficial to others and important to society as a whole.

Be Innovative With the Environment

Mukesh Ambani is one of the many who believe that taking care of nature is a way to success. With his capital, he can do more for the environment. He has planted trees using seawater and many other organic plants around his refineries. Over 100,000 mango trees that produce 110 different species of mango can be found in this green belt. The orchard is irrigated by wastewater and desalinated water from the refinery. It also grows other goods like guavas, pomegranates, oranges, and cashews. Mukesh Ambani says that an entrepreneur must be able to look at things from a different angle. An entrepreneur should understand that contributing to the environment is necessary. We use our resources and have even exhausted some of them; we are in a condition of ecological breakdown in India and the whole world.

Always Look at the Positive Side

Mukesh Ambani believes that an entrepreneur is a person who spreads positivity. Entrepreneurs should always be optimistic, as they are the ones making decisions in the company. Optimists have healthier outlooks and tend to live longer than their pessimistic counterparts. They are less susceptible to the adverse effects of illness, fatigue, and depression. Mukesh Ambani says that as an entrepreneur, you must ignore the cynics. He says to fill your ears with "melodies of optimism" and go on and take a risk. An entrepreneur finds a big problem and solves it. If you want to be an entrepreneur, focus on the facts, and eliminate your negative ideas for more upbeat, realistic ones. Get rid of the negative mindset: It's simple to become caught up in a negative thought cycle.

Have Faith in the Next Generation

Mukesh Ambani has been saying that believing in the future generation is essential in today's world. He motivates everyone to create a structure for the company that will outlast the leaders. He says that any organisation must have faith in its future generation, that they will do even better than the current one. Mukesh invested approximately $35 billion into Jio, enabling it to enter the mobile phone sector and rise to the top four companies, making his statements appear prophetic. It is ideas and innovation that will lead the world and not capital. Mukesh Ambani, the founder of Reliance Jio, has said that it is time for every business person to hand over their business to the future generation to work better for the country. Given that the younger generation is leading activities in the digital sphere and are also the biggest consumers of digital material, the future for Jio appears promising. These people are "digital natives," members of a generation raised in a world with constant digital input.

Be Empathetic and Look Out for Your Customers

Empathy is one of Mukesh Ambani's guiding values. He thinks that all business people ought to have empathy. Empathy entails kindness and sharing with every person in our company and the rest of the world. He said that the "We Care" approach encompassed all stakeholders, including shareholders, financiers, investors, employees, partners, and society. When Ambani discovered that the majority of cell phones and other goods were either made in China or were prohibitively expensive, then Jio understood that the 24,000 price tag was too costly for new phones and that a different solution was required. The designed team then came up with lowest-cost Jio phones. Ambani attended to his customers and their needs, and suggests everyone should do the same.

❑

Top Motivational / Inspiring Quotes

1. A goal is a dream with a deadline.
2. A third track running at that time, apart from academics and the fun stuff, was that my father shared with me his passion for business and entrepreneurship from very early on.
3. Advertising is only evil when it advertises evil things
4. All of us, in a sense, struggle continuously all the time, because we never get what we want.
5. Any business that has the sole purpose of making money is not worth doing.
6. As long as we place millions of Indians at the canter of our thought process, as long as we think of their welfare, their future, their opportunities for self-realization we are on the right track.
7. As long as we place millions of Indians at the centre of our thought process, as long as we think of their

welfare, their future, their opportunities for self-realisation we are on the right track.

8. As long as you've got your courage of conviction, it works for you. I think that the same applies, too, even where you don't, because, in today's world, financial resources are the least important.
9. At Reliance, we have always believed in investing in the businesses of the future and in investing in talent.
10. Be content to act, and leave the talking to others.
11. Broadband and digital services will no longer be a luxury item – a scarce commodity – to be rationed amongst the privileged few.
12. Business must serve a larger societal purpose.
13. By that time - the early '70s - Vimal was a fairly successful textile brand. So everybody expected me to do textile engineering. I shocked them by saying that I would go to IIT.
14. China and India will, separately and together, unleash an explosion of demand.
15. Courage is being scared to death, but saddling up anyway.
16. Creative without strategy is called art. Creative with strategy is called advertising.
17. Dance to your music and take some risks in life, because it is often the risk-taker who changes the course of history... and contribute to the well-being of millions of lives.
18. Digital life and digital services are a multi-wave business.
19. Do a job and do it well.

20. Dominance in the world will come only from how well a nation can cope with economic realism and towards that India must work, must find its place under the sun.
21. Essentially, whoever is successful, whoever is going to do things that make a difference, is going to be talked about.
22. Even when I was in high school, I used to spend long hours at the office on weekends.
23. Everybody has equal opportunity and I think that is true for everything.
24. Expect the best. Prepare for the worst. Capitalize on what comes.
25. Failure defeats losers, failure inspires winners.
26. Fill your years and minds with melodies of optimism.
27. For India can grow, prosper, flourish only if they grow, prosper, flourish. We cannot grow by any esoteric strategies.
28. For my father, life was uni-dimensional. Reliance was his life. Yet, some of my most vivid memories are about spending time with him. However busy he may have been, whatever the pressure, Sunday was for his wife and kids. I try to do the same with my family.
29. Formal education will make you a living; self-education will make you a fortune.
30. Good ideas come from bad ideas, but only if there are enough of them.
31. Have the end in mind and every day make sure your working towards it

32. I am a big believer that technology shapes mankind.
33. I am a big believer that whatever has gone lies in the past. You should only learn from it, and you should only look at the present and the future. That's been my father's philosophy and mine as well.
34. I am personally a big believer that technology is the biggest driver of human development, and if you can use technology to benefit people, then that's the best business you can have.
35. I believe, 50 years from now, when you write history, one technology that would have changed human civilization is going to be the mobile Internet.
36. I did chemical engineering because it was supposed to be the future.
37. I don't think that ambition should not be in the dictionary of entrepreneurs. But our ambition should be realistic.
38. I generally think that I should only speak by action and not by words.
39. I guess when you are left on your own, you find your true potential.
40. I have always believed that technology drives human civilization's endeavour and progress.
41. I have turned into a big nature fan as well... I can afford it more today. These childhood influences have shaped me into what I am today.
42. I remember my father never came to our school even once.
43. I think that money can do very little. And this has been my experience all across.

44. I think that our fundamental belief is that for us growth is a way of life and we have to grow at all times.
45. I used to spend long hours at the office on weekends.
46. I wanted to pursue chemical engineering because I thought it was the future.
47. Identify your problems but give your power and energy to solutions.
48. If it is Asia today then the African continent cannot be far behind.
49. If there are some losses that you take, then we're all big boys - we shouldn't be crying.
50. If you can't feed a team with two pizzas, it's too large
51. If your ship doesn't come in, swim out to meet it!
52. In my father's language: To create something out of nothing. That possibility exists in India even in old-world sectors like agriculture.
53. In the energy business, we give 2% of the world's petrol, diesel, and aviation fuel.
54. In the journey of an entrepreneur, the most important thing is self-belief and the ability to convert that belief into reality.
55. It is important to achieve our goals, but not at any cost.
56. It is important to remember, there are no overnight successes.
57. Logic will get you from A to B. Imagination will take you everywhere.
58. Mahatma Gandhi's dream of self-reliance can be attained by making use of the Internet and technology.

59. Mobile internet will be the single-most defining technology of this century for human development.
60. My big advantage was to have my father accept me as first-generation.
61. My obsession is with technology and how it can improve human life. In my view, what we have seen in the last 300 years is only a trailer.
62. My view is to give everyone the space to grow in his way.
63. Nobody had anticipated that chemicals were the direction in which Reliance was headed.
64. Now that economic realism has finally arrived in India, the future lies in becoming a strong economic power.
65. One day your life will flash before your eyes. Make sure it is worth watching.
66. One does not discover new lands without consenting to lose sight of the shore for a very long time.
67. Our childhood was different. I guess when you are left on your own; you find your true potential. I remember my father never came to our school even once. Nevertheless, he was hugely interested in our all-round development for which he did some amazing things.
68. Our established businesses of hydrocarbons, energy, and petrochemicals pretty much run on their own, with their proven leaders. This has helped me focus almost exclusively on two things: Firstly, new businesses. And secondly, institutionalising what I call the Reliance Management System.

69. Our purchasing power, our economic strength, our marketplace all depends on the prosperity of our people.
70. Paying attention to simple little things that most men neglect makes a few men rich.
71. Poor people have a big TV. Rich people have a big library.
72. Profit or loss is not guaranteed. That depends on the consumer and depends on the product. That's a risk that business people take.
73. Relationship and trust are the bedrock of life.
74. Reliance has built a refinery-led energy business and a materials business.
75. So, these were the four components of my upbringing – the academic stiff where I was left to myself, Mahendrabhai, my father's passion for creating Reliance and that last piece was his deep links with the family.
76. Stopping advertising to save money is like stopping your watch to save time.
77. Success is walking from failure to failure with no loss of enthusiasm.
78. Success likes yourself, liking what you do, and liking how you do it.
79. The business has only two functions–marketing and innovation.
80. The function of leadership is to produce more leaders, not more followers.
81. The important thing which I've learned is how you do not give up because you never succeed in the first attempt.

82. The organizational architecture is really that a centipede walks on a hundred legs and one or two don't count. So if I lose one or two legs, the process will go on, the organization will go on, the growth will go on.
83. The regulator's job is not to guarantee us a profit, however much we cry.
84. The regulator's job is to first make sure that the country goes forward and then make sure that the consumer goes forward.
85. The world has moved to the power of ideas.
86. To build our new refinery in 60 percent of the time it took to build our first, we are training 20,000 people in a new generation of welding technology in six months.
87. Today I see a billion people as a billion potential consumers, an opportunity to generate value for them and to make a return for myself Tune out the critics and cynics.
88. Until my father brought me into Reliance, I was pretty sure that I wanted to study in a U.S. university: hopefully, a little bit of time, either work at the World Bank or teach as a professor.
89. We all get into the business, and we take a risk in terms of putting capital.
90. We are now investing in each of our businesses to achieve substantial earnings growth in the future and create further value for millions of our shareholders.
91. We are using new technologies in meaningful ways.
92. We are what we repeatedly do. Excellence then is not an act but a habit.

93. We call it infectious impatience. That's his hallmark and we are trying to inculcate it in the entire organization. Infectious impatience. So that thing not only gets done but gets done in double-quick time.
94. What the mind of man can conceive and believe, it can achieve.
95. When you see restructuring or separations in a family (firm), value has almost always been destroyed. This is the first case where value has been enhanced. In that way, it has been a win-win ending.
96. Why will I not give free service to my customers to get them used to mobile Internet, and to get every small town and village to use it? Everybody does promotions. In the internet world, free is normal.
97. You have to manage the money. Particularly with market economies.
98. You have to realise that you can't do anything.
99. You may have a great product, but if your bottom line goes bust, then that's it.
100. You will need to be dedicated, single-minded, and there is no substitute for hard work.

❑